THE MAIN COURSE

Also By Chuck Morgue

The Horns Of Evangelina

THE MAIN COURSE

CHUCK MORGUE

HOUSE OF MORGUE

2009

THE MAIN COURSE

Cover and author photography: Victoria "Viy" Nosser
Art direction: Chuck Morgue

Published by House Of Morgue

For contact information visit:
www.houseofmorgue.com

ISBN 978-0-578-01140-0

FIRST EDITION

10 9 8 7 6 5 4 3 2 1

Acknowledgements

I would like to first thank my family - Fallon, Izzy, Rowan, Lex, and Helena (be seeing you soon) - for putting up with me and the ridiculous amount of arrogant shit that I put them through while researching and writing this book (I love you guys).

Very special thanks goes to Dr. Joseph Suglia, my brother in blood, who has provided me with much appreciated criticism, guidance, friendship and inspiration (I'll have a plate of barbeque waiting for you when we get together).

To Heather Christian, for making incredible music and allowing me to feature her in this story (I promised not to treat you badly).

I enthusiastically thank Victoria "Viy" Nosser for lending her superb photographic skills to the artwork for this book (I had a bloody good time, lady).

Thank you to all of my friends who have supported me in my decision to alienate them and write into the wee hours of the night (Now if you would all return my calls).

And of course, a huge thanks to Christopher Walken and Johnny Depp, whose films have delighted me for years and without whom this book would have never been written (When you read this book, you'll understand).

I would also like to thank the following people for their support of my work, and the warm reception they gave for my first novel *The Horns Of Evangelina*: Justin Talarski, Christopher Robin, Dax Riggs, Robert Johnson, Darl Herman, Alaric Snow, Matt Bonin, Jade Reynolds, Michael Emsminger, Ryan Newman, my brother Billy, my sister Becky, my Aunt Pauline, Brent Wiggins, Perry Frith, Jason Ourso, Trey Harris, Juicy Jones, Danielle Saxon, Tosha Woody, Jamie Etheridge, and the rest of you who I may have neglected to mention. I hope you all enjoy this book just as much, if not more so.

And thank you, curious reader, for making the decision of wasting your time with this book. I hope it will make you laugh. Make you cry. Make you hungry. And make you hungry for more. Bon appétit.

THE MAIN COURSE

Edible, adj.: Good to eat, and wholesome to digest, as a worm to a toad, a toad to a snake, a snake to a pig, a pig to a man, and a man to a worm.

Ambrose Bierce

CONTENTS

HORS D'OEUVRES

THE DONOVAN RUSHING PHILOSOPHY OF COOKING

There is no such thing as a perfect meal.

No matter how well-prepared a meal may seem to be, no matter how delicious, how absurdly ravishing, it can always be better.

And that is the cruel dilemma of being a great, a so-called great, chef.

You can always do it better. There is always something new and different to explore.

And this simple little fact scares the literal shit out of most of us. Myself included.

To sweat over a stove, bones aching, nerves throbbing, throat sore from screaming over the din of mass hysteria and riot that is often mistaken for a restaurant kitchen, to spend every waking moment thinking about food, and how to cook it, how you cooked it last night, how you fucked it up for a moment several weeks ago, how you forgot to order fresh scallops from the market until now, and you've only got fifteen minutes until the doors open and those first few customers take their seats, and you just know they are going to want the poached scallops, because Rushing's is one of the top restaurants in town and the scallops are one of your specialties and it's been one of those days where nothing seems to be going right, where there is possible disaster lurking around every corner in a kitchen with corners out the ass, to stand there, and sweat over that stove, it never fails, the one thought you get is that you could do this better.

Or worse still, someone else could.

I've been doing this for thirty-plus years. And it never gets any easier. But when you have a passion for something, a fervency this intense, nothing can spoil it.

2

Nothing can take it away.

Even if you find that actually, no, you could not do this better.

It's not that you are perfect. Or imperfect, for that matter. It's just the simple inarguable truth that you are as good as you are going to get. You have reached your peak. And it is just a matter of time before someone else notices, and passes you up. Leaves you behind. Just a matter of time before someone does it better than you, and they win.

And what can you do? Do you hang up your chef's jacket, go home and watch a marathon of *Highway To Heaven* reruns on a bloated retro-TV channel?

No. You cook. And you keep cooking until the day you die. Because it's all you *can* do. It's all you know how to do.

And when you are not cooking, in the small amount of free time this profession bestows upon you irregularly, then you can linger on those thoughts of what you did wrong, how to do it right, how to do it better.

And of course, plotting the destruction of anyone around you who you even suspect of posing the slightest little threat. You watch everyone closely. Because deep down, you know they hate you. And you know that if they should ever get the chance, they will knock you aside and take it all away. Everything you have worked so hard for. The house, the cars, the restaurant, the television show, even your precious set of Global knives, they will take them and laugh at you as you crawl on your filthy, tired knees, grasping for control of a hopeless situation.

And so you watch them. All of them. You never take your eyes off of them.

And out the corner of your eye you see a man, and he looks urgent, suspicious. You stare him down, you watch his every move. You just know this is it, this is when it happens. When the shit hits the kitchen fan. And he gives you a message. A message that changes your entire world for the rest of the evening.

The scallops have arrived.

ALL YOU NEED TO KNOW FOR NOW

So you want to know what it takes to be a professional chef in this day and age? Well, I suppose you have come to the right place. I have been cooking for over fifty years, and doing it professionally for over thirty.

I would assume that I know a thing or two about this life and work. But if I am to use myself as the example, since I reasonably know myself better than I know someone else, to give you a proper examination of this culinary world, then I should probably start at the beginning.

And so welcome to 1945.

I was born Rudolph Rushing into an eccentric little family in Queens, New York. Of course you all know me now as Donovan

Rushing, but I did not take that name until later. As a boy, I was simply Rudy.

My parents were immigrants to America, my mother from Scotland and my father from Germany. They were the owners of Rushing's Bakery, a modest little shop in the Astoria neighborhood. It should come as no surprise that I was practically raised in that bakery. My family spent more time there than in our own apartment a few blocks away.

I was an obedient kid, for the most part. My father had strict rules, and was strict to enforce them. But my mother, she was a little more engaged in the act of living. New York had so much to offer. From the theaters and museums to the restaurants and shopping. Now, we did not have very much money, but we were occasionally comfortable, and my mother spoiled me when she could.

When I was just eight years old, my mother took me downtown to a talent agency which had posted a notice looking for kids for locally produced television programs. I was somehow lucky enough to get accepted, being a cute enough kid I suppose, and I was placed as an extra in a few unmemorable programs. Although I did get to meet Jerry Lewis and Dean Martin briefly, when I was brought in to appear in a comedic sketch with them for some show produced by a major toothpaste company. That was one of the highlights of my childhood.

My mother, filled with equal parts pride and delusion, expected my dumb luck to continue, signing me up for theatre classes and taking me to even more auditions. And while I did learn quite a bit from the barely-qualified acting coaches and small time directors, my heart just was not really in it. It was helping my father at the bakery that gave me the most joy.

While other kids were reading Superman comic books and going to baseball games, I was trying to perfect my bakers' hands, working on cakes and pies and muffins and breads.

It was the process that thrilled me. Taking raw ingredients, much of which would make you sick if you ate them by themselves, and mixing them just right, and cooking them at the proper temperature for the proper amount of time, and coming out at the end with a delicious work of art.

It was like a miracle. It was like magic.

As a teenager, I only excelled at my talents. I was running the bakery by myself on some days. And doing a far better job than my father, in my own opinion.

It was in 1958 that I got my first break. I was fifteen and I was offered a job as a pastry chef at a local restaurant. The restaurant manager was a friend of my father, and had found my skills admirable. I don't recall the name of the restaurant because I was only there a few months, and the place has been closed for decades now. What I do remember is being terrified. It was my first time in an actual professional kitchen, with a full brigade of cooks. I found myself in a situation that would require a lot of communication, which required talking. And this was something that made me a little uncomfortable.

You see, what most people did not realize about me was that being raised by a Scottish mother and a German father, strange accents and the occasional butchering of the English language, this left me with a peculiar vocal quality. While my accent was almost pure Queens, my tone was strong and monotone, straight and dry, and I frequently found myself getting stuck on a thought, causing me to pause midsentence for apparently no reason, and put unnecessary stress on random words.

It was one of the reasons I had given up acting as a kid. I imagined that my peculiar speech pattern would eventually prevent me from getting real acting jobs in motion pictures as I got older. It's funny now to think about it, considering it was the erratic nature of my voice that helped me garner attention later in life, as I understand it I am one of the most impersonated personalities alive today, but back then, as a young man, it bothered me a little. But as it turned out, most of the cooks and restaurant staff I worked with found it amusing, and I eventually quit worrying about it.

I embraced my strange, little voice.

It was at my first real job that I earned the friendship of Carlos Estrada, the sous chef, who was twenty at the time. His family had moved to New York from Spain when he was seven years old, and he had started working in kitchens when he was thirteen, washing dishes, learning what he could, and quickly moved up to the sous chef position in only six years. Of course, this restaurant was not an overtly professional establishment (they had gone through five head chefs during Carlos' time there, and changed restaurant names twice), but Carlos was an absolute madman in the kitchen. And he was a good friend to me, probably because we were closer in age than most of the other kitchen staff. I was there for almost four weeks when Carlos helped me convince the manager to move me up to line cook. I was making real food now, and I was doing very well. He was hoping to get the head chef's job, but after I was working the line for a few months he received an offer from Dans La Merde, a more high cuisine French restaurant in Manhattan.

Dans La Merde had recently undergone major renovations, both structural and managerial, and was hiring a whole new kitchen staff. Carlos accepted the job almost instantly, as being executive chef was his ultimate goal, and Dans La Merde would be a perfect chance to build a reputation for himself.

Carlos was now one of the youngest executive chefs in New York, especially for a restaurant of this caliber. It only took him a week to get me brought in with him.

And I had no idea why, but I was offered the job as his sous chef.

It should go without saying that I was a little hesitant at first. I barely knew anything about real cooking, having only been doing it professionally for several months. Cakes and breads I had been making for years, but now we were talking about *emincé de volaille sauce Roquefort* and *yeux cuit's à la vapeur d'agnueau* and meals with foie gras. I didn't even know that these dishes existed a few months ago. Carlos assured me that things would be okay. The restaurant had two weeks to prepare and get used to the kitchen, and Carlos said he would teach me enough to get by.

And he did. And just as before, I picked things up quickly. While it seemed to me a bit unfair that I had moved ahead so quickly, on the basis of my personality more than my skills, which were not shabby at all in their own right, the other line cooks warmed up to me quickly, and I knew this was an important opportunity. This was my first real lesson.

Grab what you are offered, without hesitation, and do not look back.

That's what I did, and have continued to do since.

Seven years I worked under Carlos in the kitchen at Dans La Merde. The restaurant's reputation grew, and we were often visited by a number of celebrity guests. From President Johnson to Audrey Hepburn and Mel Ferrer, who were regulars. When a celebrity came in, we couldn't wait to step out of the boiling heat of the kitchen to meet them and ask about their meal, did they enjoy it. And they were usually just as thrilled to meet us.

Our food was that god damned good.

But it was one important guest who changed my life. Yes, I've told this story hundreds of times, everyone knows it by now, but for the uninformed I'll delve into it once again. It's one of my favorites.

It was in August of 1965. On Friday. It was the thirteenth. Yeah, I know. Strange.

It was one of the busiest nights we'd had all week, about five hundred meals, it was absolute chaos. If we stopped for even a minute to breathe, we were up to our shoulders in the weedy shit. When we received word that one of the tables wanted to meet us, we politely declined, knowing full well how integral it was that Carlos and myself keep moving in the kitchen. When the table sent a second request, we declined again, Carlos getting a little rude with the waiter. The waiter, quite a bit nervous, headed back out to the dining room. It was less than a minute later that he stepped back through into the kitchen, obviously concerned.

"I really think one of you needs to get out to this guy's table," he said, nearly crying.

"Which table," Carlos asked.

The waiter said it was table thirty. The customer had ordered the *aile de raie aux câpres*, or skate wing with capers. I had prepared that meal. But I was overloaded at my station, so Carlos begrudgingly agreed to step out for a quick meet and greet.

Things were fine for about five minutes, and then Carlos came running back into the kitchen.

"Rudy, it's fucking Frank Sinatra."

I stopped cooking whatever it was I was cooking, and looked at Carlos.

"He loved the meal. He wants to meet you."

I couldn't move. Frank Sinatra.

"Rudy…"

I wanted to pass out. Frank Sinatra. Wanted to meet me. How do you not pass out in such a situation?

Then, before I could say anything, behind Carlos, through the kitchen door, Frank Sinatra walked right into the kitchen. He walked right past Carlos, right towards me. In real life, you have to understand,

14

Frank Sinatra looks like a real gangster. I should know, they ate in our restaurant regularly. Sinatra is intimidating, frightening. He had a smile on his face, but there was that glint in his eye. Something that seemed to say "Look at me wrong, and you'll spend the night at the bottom of the river."

"Chef Donnie, my meal was immaculate."

That is what Frank Sinatra said to me. His meal was immaculate. But Donnie. He called me Donnie. Carlos later told me that Sinatra had put away a few drinks that night, and that the name Rudy had somehow turned into Donnie in the few minutes since Carlos told him my name.

"Thank you, sir." It was all I could say.

He shook my hand, and said "I'll be back. I hope you'll cook for me again."

"Thank you, sir." Still all I could get out of my throat.

He yelled out a collective thank you

to the entire kitchen, then he left. It took about five minutes before we realized that everyone in the kitchen was just standing there. Doing nothing.

Robert, the dishwasher, finally broke the silence. "Way to go, Chef Donnie!"

The kitchen erupted with laughter, and then a light applause. I felt my face turn red with embarrassment. Then, it was back to work.

And because of the impromptu break, we were behind. Very behind. The remaining three hours of service were horrible. We screwed up half the orders. But we didn't care. Not that night.

After that, I was Chef Donnie. It started as an inside joke, then other people, friends of Sinatra we assumed, would arrive and ask that their meal be prepared by Chef Donnie. I obliged, never correcting anyone. When the *Times* showed up to interview us in November, I gave my name as Donovan Rushing. Carlos suggested the name, saying he took it from a popular singer at the time.

That's how it started. One immaculate

meal, several dry martinis, one mistaken name, and I became a different person. This was when my career truly began.

Of course there is a downside to all the excitement and good times. A kitchen in the heat of the night is a rotten place to be. There are a lot of egos running around back there, and it doesn't take long for a heated argument to spill into the back alley, bloody fists swinging away.

It was one of these situations that shook things up quite a bit at Dans La Merde. This story is one of my least favorites. Or at least the first of many to come.

Christmas Eve, 1965, at the restaurant, is where it started. We were having a ridiculously brutal time in the kitchen. Barry Greenfield, our restaurant manager had taken a few days off, and on this night he slipped in with his family for dinner, and so we had to give their orders a little special attention. Which would have been fine under any other circumstance, only Barry had brought along a total party of seventeen heads. And the dining room was now completely full. In all, I believe we did maybe six hundred fifty meals.

Anyway, Barry, our manager, had brought his family in. It was in part a celebration for his youngest daughter, Elizabeth, who had completed law school earlier in the month. She was twenty-six, unconventionally attractive, and when Carlos walked out to greet them, she caught his eye.

And naturally, he caught hers.

Sometime before they left, Carlos had managed to get Elizabeth's phone number, and within days they were seeing each other. This was all very discreet, of course. Barry was a decent enough manager, but we'd heard horror stories of his disapproval of his daughters' boyfriends. He was a very old fashioned sort of guy, and had a classic ferocious temper. It was pretty obvious that he would not take very kindly to his baby girl involving herself with a sweaty Spaniard who slaved away in a kitchen for a living.

Barry only managed the restaurant because he was retired. Earlier, it was said, he was a real estate investor, and a

18

successful one at that. He took the job at Dans La Merde just to be around his good friend Patrick McHale, the owner of the restaurant.

Anyway, Carlos was quite taken by Elizabeth. She would drop in to visit her father, and when he was too busy she would slip back to the kitchen and out the back door into the alley. Carlos would look at me, I would roll my eyes and nod my head, he'd say "five minutes" and head out the door after her. Fifteen minutes later, if we were lucky, Carlos and Elizabeth would come back inside. Carlos would head for his station, and Elizabeth would slip back out through the dining room to tell her father goodnight, and she would be gone.

And this worked. Barry never suspected a thing. For a while.

It was in April that the Great Fight of '66 occurred. It was a Saturday night, we were being crushed with orders in the usual fashion. We were holding up well enough, but Barry had not shown up, and the dining room was in a bit of chaos. We were a little worried since Carlos admitted that he had not heard from Elizabeth that day. They hardly went several hours without at least a phone call or something. I thank the Lord now that there were no cell phones back then. Carlos would have never gotten any work done at all.

At a quarter to nine, we became aware of a commotion in the dining room. Carlos was getting behind on his orders, so I took a peek out the kitchen door. There were a few men arguing, and it took a moment to realize it was Barry and Patrick McHale. Then I saw Elizabeth, crying behind her father, yelling and begging to him about something. Everything just clicked in my head, and I turned to Carlos.

"You might want to get out of here."

Carlos just looked at me, questioningly.

"Barry's out there," I said. "I think he knows."

Carlos turned pale, then walked up to take a look. He was just in time to see Barry turn and throw his vocal tantrum at Elizabeth. She squealed in terror. The next thing I knew, Carlos had bolted out of the kitchen, practically leaping across patrons' tables, and pulled Barry away.

"Barry, we can talk about this."

No sooner did the words leave his lips, Carlos was falling to the ground, Barry tearing into him at full force.

"You son of a bitch!" "My little girl!" "Spanish pervert!"

This was the sort of thing you could hear over the grunts and growls and punches, and the screams from the other guests. Barry was in his fifties, but he had the stamina of a twenty year old prize fighter. Carlos was an overworked cook in a hot, exhausting restaurant.

It was not much of a fight. Carlos held his own for a few minutes, and got in a few good punches. But Barry got more. It was all over in under two minutes. Carlos was unconscious on the dining room floor, and Barry returned to arguing with Elizabeth. She said nothing to him, just walked past him and knelt down on the floor to tend to Carlos. Barry just stared down at them in disgust, and left a few minutes later.

The medics arrived and pretty soon Carlos and Elizabeth were gone and it was back to service for the rest of us.

Patrick McHale called a meeting the next day, informing us that Barry and Carlos had been let go. He would not tolerate this level of behavior at Dans La Merde. A couple of cooks taking a fight into the alley or freezer was one thing, but to have such a scene in the middle of the dining room was inexcusable. Then McHale approached me.

"You want the head chef position?"

As always, I smiled and said "Yes, sir."

"It's yours."

He shook my hand. Thomas, one of the line cooks who had shown some promise, was elevated to sous chef, and that was fine with me.

Donovan Rushing. Head Chef. At Dans La Merde. Wow. It was all very unexpected. But I ran with it. What other choice did I have, really?

It was a few weeks later we found out that Carlos had accepted the executive chef position at Feuchte Scheide, a relatively new restaurant on the other side of Manhattan. I went to visit with him, and he was glad I was now running the kitchen at Dans La Merde. He joked that now we could actually compete with one another. He was doing well at Feuchte Scheide, but it was obvious to me that he wasn't quite the same. He had allowed a personal problem to conflict with his professional life. He continued dating that girl. They eventually married.

Life goes on.

It's strange for me to look back to those times. I had covered so much ground in so little time, all because people generally liked me. And my cooking. So many people would later spend their money at a culinary school, to attain some amount of credibility before hitting the ground. I just smiled and shook hands and said "Yes, sir," taking whatever job was offered to me.

And now, I am in my sixties, with seven restaurants, a long-running television cooking show, the best manager anyone could ask for, and more money than I know what to do with. And for the life of me, I really don't have any idea what I did to deserve any of this. Sometimes, I truly feel like the luckiest man in the world.

I get up every morning, I let my two cats (Black Max and White Max) out for an hour or so, I drive my BMW through Beverley Hills, and I spend a few hours prepping and taping *The Main Course With Donovan Rushing*. I do some interviews, work on some recipes, even do a little moderate acting work (my "More flute!" skit mocking the rock band Jethro Tull on *Saturday Night Live* in 2000 is something of a cult phenomenon now).

Yes, I really have made it. And when I look back to the mid 1960s, and I realize just how little I knew back then, and how many changes I'd see in the world and in my life, it is humbling. I envy that young man, Rudy Rushing, Chef Donnie, who had nothing to lose and everything to gain.

My cell phone rings.

It's Gordon Hessler, my manager. My producer. With his distractingly thick

German accent.

"Donnie, where the hell are you?"

I take a look around. I am sitting on a bench downtown.

"Nowhere," I say. "What's going on?"

"You were supposed to be at the studio a half hour ago. What have you been doing?"

I look at my watch. "Shit. I'm on my way. I'll be there in a few minutes."

I hang up the phone, I get up and I run. I have no idea where my car is. I have no idea why I was sitting downtown alone. *Was I alone?* I was talking to someone, I think. About my childhood or some shit.

I don't see anyone who may have been listening, so I suppose I wasn't talking. Just thinking to myself. For some reason.

In over thirty years of hosting my own cooking show, I have only been late for production about ten times. And all in the last eight weeks. Maybe I'm not getting enough rest. Maybe someone is coming in and resetting my clocks, throwing me off balance, gunning for my job.

I'll have to look into it. Worry about it later. The studio is twenty minutes away. I've got ten minutes to get there. Everyone is going to be angry with me. But I don't care.

I'm just hoping that nobody steals my car.

FILMED IN FRONT OF A LIVE STUDIO AUDIENCE

The studio is a house of stark raving lunatics and epileptic chimpanzees when I step through the large red doors leading in from the western end, allowing my shoes to slip from my feet.

"I need shoes and pants *NOW*," I yell out to nobody in particular. "Socks are optional. I am in a hurry here."

"You got that right." Dean Prescott, the director for the show. An Englishman, he got his start directing cooking programs in Great Britain, before getting this job a year ago though the Network. He's pissed, that is easy to see. He doesn't even take notice when I drop my pants to the floor. "Where the fuck have you been, Donovan?"

27

"I lost track of time, Dean. I'm old. It happens now and then." I am grinning in my sly manner. One thing I like about Dean Prescott, he does not bullshit around. It doesn't matter if you are Donovan Rushing, Elvis Presley, or a goddamn mailman, when you fuck up, Dean will set you straight.

"I can't do this much longer," Dean tells me. "I can only hold off the audience, the crew and the fucking producers for so long, and I just don't think you are worth it anymore."

"Well, I hope I can prove you wrong, Dean."

"So do I."

He just stares at me through his small round spectacles, then storms off. "Five minutes," he calls out.

Jimmie, a red-haired production assistant, walks up to me with pants and shoes. "This is all we have available, Mr. Rushing."

The pants are a horrid shade of green,

28

and look to be a few sizes too big.

"Don't they keep wardrobe here for me," I ask him.

"No sir, they said you always just wear whatever you show up in."

He's right. I have always been more comfortable cooking in the clothes I've worn all day. I even quit wearing that damn chef coat years ago, although my manager keeps trying to push it on me again.

"What happened?" Jimmie asks.

"Excuse me?"

"Your pants…"

"Oh," I say. "I ran over from Continental Park, and took a detour through a gutter."

I hate Los Angeles. No, let me restate that.

I really fucking hate Los Angeles. New York is where I'm from, where I belong. My restaurant is there for Christ's sake. The important one anyway.

Everyone at the Network, and my manager, decided it would be in my best interests to relocate myself and the show to the west coast. And so I did. And here we all have been for going on twelve years.

I slip into the green pants, comfortable with the fact that my lower half will be obscured behind the work station and the stove top. I allow the make up lady, I think she's a lady, I've never been completely sure in the six years she has worked here, to touch up my face a little. I attach the small microphone to my shirt, and the tiny, almost invisible earpiece into my left ear, since most of the shots will be head on or on my right profile. I take a deep breath. Melissa, my assistant, walks up with my glass of wine, Pinot Noir as always, I take a healthy mouthful and swallow, then step out on the stage to greet my adoring fans.

One hundred and twenty food lovers, tourists, journalists and absolute nobodies cheer and applaud from their seats in the studio. I nod, smile, wave. I say thank you, and point to a few people, no one in particular, and when Dean Prescott, the director, speaks through my invisible earpiece, "Donovan, we are good to go," I take my place behind the cooking station.

And it begins.

Hello, everyone. I'm Donovan Rushing. Welcome to The Main Course.

A quick swell of applause from the audience.

You know, I was having a conversation a few days ago with a good friend of mine, and at my age I hate to name drop so I won't say it was Wolfgang Puck...

Small bit of laughter from the audience.

... and we ended up talking about how hard it is to find really good French food in Los Angeles. Sure, there are a few notable restaurants, but honestly, if you are not in the mood for Asian cuisine, or Mexican, or fried chicken with a side of waffles...

A little more laughter.

...then you are really up the proverbial creek. Unless of course you are vegetarian, then you can always just graze down at the park or something.

This is how it goes. I try, hard as I can, to be entertaining, because it's what they pay me for. But, really I can't stand it. I'm not an entertainer, I'm a chef. I'm not Emeril Lagasse. I'm not Rachael Ray. I'm Donovan Rushing. Cook. Chef. Restaurateur. My restaurants bring in more money in one month than the producers of this show make in one year. And let me tell you, the producers are not complaining about their paychecks.

Today, you are in for a treat. I am going to show you how to make one of my favorite French meals. This one actually goes back to my days at Dans La Merde, in Manhattan. I included this dish in my Dans La Merde Cookbook, *but I have never made it on television before. This dish, it might look a little difficult, but really, it's not. You just need a little patience, and a free afternoon. I am going to prepare* mignons de porc à l'ail.

The audience erupts in applause. This

was one of my rare signature dishes back in the day.

Now, my materials, my mise en place, *are already organized for me. So at home you will want to be sure everything you need is positioned for your personal convenience.*

Of course, like every production day, the staff cooks have set up my station for me. They have been thoroughly trained to have my space organized to my exact specifications. This is crucial to any chef, professional or otherwise. *Mise en place* pretty much means "everything in it's place." You've got your shit where it belongs. Your cooking tools, your ingredients, your paper towels, everything. This is different for everyone. Everyone is an individual, so they have individual preferences on how their cooking space is set up. If something is wrong, the cutting board is sitting at the wrong the angle, the tongs are in the drawer instead of to the immediate left of my seasonings, anything like this, it can throw off the delicate equilibrium of the cooking process, condemning a meal to the Big Waste Bucket in the sky.

We're going to start by preheating the oven to 350. We're going to need to make some garlic confit before starting on the pork. What you'll need is two big beautiful heads of garlic.

I reach to my right, and remove the garlic from a ceramic bowl.

God, I love garlic. Don't you?

The audience responds, positively. They know how to play this game.

Break the garlic into cloves. But be careful to leave the skin intact.

"Pick it up a little," the director's voice whispers into my earpiece. I make no response, I simply process the command and execute the task. I reach for the aluminum foil.

Now you're going to wrap the garlic in a small sheet of aluminum foil. Drown the garlic in a few tablespoons of olive oil, and close up the foil. Then into the oven for a half hour.

I do everything that I say, and I say

everything that I do. Tests have shown that much of the viewing audience is a little slow to pick up on things, and gets distracted. Lawyers for the Network have expressed concern that should someone at home screw up a recipe because I don't express it correctly on the show, then we could possibly be held liable for any damages they incur. I say it's bullshit, but it's their rules and not mine.

When the garlic cloves are done, let them cool a while before removing the skins. Now for me, through the miracle of television production, my cloves are ready. You'll want to use a fork to mash up about half of the garlic cloves.

I reach to my right for the fork, and find empty countertop instead.

My body comes to a dead halt. I say nothing for several seconds.

"What's going on, Donovan?" The voice in my ear.

My fork, um, seems to have been misplaced.

"Look in the drawer."

35

Of course, I know it is probably in there, but I can't bring myself to look. The fork was supposed to be on the countertop, on the right, in front of the knife rack. Which I now notice is missing as well.

Where the fuck are my knives?

The little old ladies in the audience give an audible gasp. Pardon my French, you old goodie goodies, but my shit has been fucked with.

"Cut! Everybody cut," The director's voice, not in my ear, but over the intercom. Almost immediately I see him exit the little booth on the opposite side of the studio and make his way down the stairs and through an aisle in the audience towards the stage.

He walks up, opens the drawer and pulls out the fork, setting it down in it's proper location on the counter.

"What about my knives?"

"I don't know, Donovan. But I'll tell you what, when I find out who misplaced them, I'll fire them. Will that make you feel better?"

"Perhaps."

He sighs. "Donovan. You've got replacement knives in the other kitchen. Will they suffice for now?"

"I guess. But I would prefer mine. I am used to them."

"I know, but it's been a long day for everyone already. Your being late hasn't really helped."

"Dean, I'm sorry about that…"

"I don't care. Look, we have three shows to shoot. Are you good to go, or do we need to shut it down for the day?"

"I'm good."

"Are you sure?"

"Yeah. Somebody fucked with my shit."

"I know."

"That isn't supposed to happen, Dean."

"I know. I'm sorry. We'll fix it."

A staffer brings out the replacement knives. They look identical to the ones I use everyday. But I know they'll feel different.

I go back to the station. All crew members return to their positions. I watch the assistant director count down from four. I wait for the large green light on the back wall to light up.

And it starts again.

Hello, everyone. I'm Donovan Rushing. Welcome to The Main Course.

A swell of applause. Same as before.

I mostly repeat everything I said earlier, trying to give the same amount of enthusiasm. But I'm sure it's not working. They'll have to edit with the first take and hope it comes together.

I begin to explain the meal. The *mignons de porc à l'ail*. Something makes me looks over to the large plate of pork tenderloins, and I come to a stop again. Staring at the plate, I feel the grimace crawl over my face.

Jesus fucking Christ!

The director comes running out of the booth, but it's too late. I pick up the plate.

This is chicken, Goddamn it!

I throw the plate across the stage, and it shatters against a wall. Audience members, in utter shock and awe, fidget in their seats. I walk off the stage, into the spare kitchen, out of view of the audience.

Dean approaches me, cautiously this time.

"Okay, somebody has really fucked up," he says.

"You're goddamn right."

"We're shutting down. No point in pushing it."

"Somebody did this on purpose," I

39

say.

"No…"

"Yes! I'm sure of it. Somebody is trying to make me look like a fucking idiot out there!"

"Who, Donovan? Who would do that?"

"I don't know. That new kid, maybe. What's his name… Scotty."

"The production assistant?"

"Yeah," I say. "He's a little squirrelly looking."

"He's not even here today."

"Probably too ashamed to show his face…"

"Donovan." The voice comes from behind me. It's Gordon Hessler. My manager. My god damn knight in shining armor. Thank God.

I turn to him. "Gordon, I'm ready to

start losing it."

"You've already lost it," he says with a grin. "You should go home. Get some rest. We can all start fresh tomorrow."

"What about my knives? What about all of this?"

"I will handle everything."

"But…"

"Don't you trust me, Donovan?"

Of course I trust him. Gordon Hessler has been my saving grace for my entire television career. I trust him more than I trust myself sometimes.

If Gordon says he will handle something, he means it.

So I nod my head, and gather my dirty pants and shoes into a plastic bag. I wait for the audience to be cleared out, and I take my leave across the stage. Even though we did not complete show production for the day, the stage exit is the way I must leave. It's a personal thing.

On my way out I glimpse the plate I had smashed against the wall. The plate of chicken that was supposed to be pork. Well, the meat laying on the floor, it is now clearly pork.

I make a mental note. Someone replaced the meat. Someone is trying to make a fool of me. I have absolutely no doubt of that now.

But I will not go down lightly. I will not go gently in the night.

I am Donovan Rushing. Cook. Chef. Restaurateur.

And I really fucking hate this city.

DOWN AND OUT IN
DOWNTOWN L.A.

I call a cab to pick me up from the studio. Taken downtown, I locate my car. It is parked in front of Orwell's Antiquated Tomes Bookstore, just a few blocks from the park bench I found myself at earlier. I don't have any idea why I would have parked there.

The thought occurs to me that someone may have moved my car. Just to fuck with me. Then I notice something different. There is a bumper sticker on the rear fender. What the fuck?

It reads: *Motörhead Is My Co-Pilot*.

Whatever the fuck that means. But it's proof, to me, that some stupid fuck has been

43

deliberately fucking with my car. I rip the sticker off and make a mental note to look into this mad conspiracy.

I call Gordon to see if he wants to meet up for dinner. I would really like to talk to him about all of the strange things that have been happening to me. I am sure he could help me get to the bottom of it.

His voice mail is the only response:

This is Gordon Hessler. I can not be reached at the moment. I am currently engaged in serious business meeting. Leave a message or call again tomorrow.

I hang up the phone. *Serious business meeting.* Who is he kidding? The only business meeting that he could be engaged in would require me to be there. Maybe it is a secret meeting. Is Gordon working against me as well?

Sure. Why not. Fuck it.

On my own tonight, I suppose. Which is fine really. I reach into my pocket for my iPod, one of the few modern marvels that I get any enjoyment out of. It's a little digital music player, sort of like a walkman with a little computer inside. It was a Christmas gift from my good friend Carlos a few years ago. I have over three thousand songs on this thing. Mostly jazz and blues, but also a little classic country western, and a few older rock and roll standards. I have almost the entire Frank Sinatra musical catalog on this tiny plastic wonder. I put on the tiny earphones and I turn the iPod on. I find a song, and I hit play. Frank Sinatra. "We Kiss In A Shadow." One of my personal favorites.

Now, I need to find something to do. I could drive down to Napa Valley, treat myself to one of Thomas Keller's tasting menus. Or I could go to Ginza Sushiko and enjoy the fine food of Chef Masayoshi Takayama. Then again, it's highly doubtful that these chefs would be at their restaurants. I am almost never at mine. Although I do make a point to spend two weeks personally running the kitchen at Rushing's in Manhattan every October. But that is months away from now.

No, tonight I think I will have a grilled ham and cheese sandwich. I will drink a little wine. And I will rent a movie.

Something with James Stewart. *No Highway In The Sky* perhaps. It's one of his best films. That would be nice.

Yes, this is going to be a waste of a night. Which is quickly becoming more and more preferable to me. Why go out for a night on the town, when you can just sit at home. Alone. Staring at walls covered with thirty thousand dollar paintings by artists whose names you can't even pronounce.

I don't even like those god damn paintings. My art dealer, Julius, said they were good investments. So I bought them.

One of the paintings, a brightly colored portrait of Oscar Wilde. I swear to god, I have no idea why I bought it. Julius has that affect. I can't tell him No. But the painting. Sometimes, I think it's looking at me. Watching me. Trying to speak to me.

Sometimes, I think it does speak. A month ago, I walked past it, and I honestly believe it said "Nice ass." I just kept walking.

I should not have bought that painting. No, sir.

I could have bought more vintage wine. I have hundreds of bottles already. From everywhere in the world. Most are in storage in New York, but I keep a few dozen bottles here for special occasions.

Tonight is no special occasion. But that's all right. I can make exceptions.

Now don't get me wrong. I love to go out with friends and enjoy a nice evening at a fine restaurant, but the fact of the matter is that I don't have that many friends. Not in Los Angeles. I have several wonderful friends and colleagues back in New York, and more scattered around the country. Around the world, really. But here in L.A., if I'm not with Gordon, or any number of lawyers or business representatives, then I really am on my own. I've met a few chefs out here. Thomas Keller. Mario Manabe. Vania Almeida. They are all genuinely gracious individuals, but not exactly my style of people. When Wolfgang Puck is in town we get together. But to be honest, the man can really creep me out sometimes.

He is Austrian after all. You know how those people can be.

I get along fine with my assistants, handlers, and go-getters, but I can barely remember their names most of the time. And it doesn't help that Gordon is constantly, routinely firing and hiring them.

But he's been my only manager, and I his only client, for decades now. And I trust his judgment. He's almost never been wrong and he certainly has never let me down.

So what's a man to do? Get out there and make some new friends? Get over my hesitations and really see what L.A. is all about?

No. Not me. Maybe in my younger days. But now, I'm not so adventurous.

Of course I have one exception to that.

I have my secret week.

Every year, during the summer, I spend a week isolated from everyone I know. No one knows where I am or what I am doing. Not even Gordon.

I go to the same place, and do the same thing, every year. I've been doing it since 1970. And I do it because I love it. It's a special and important time for me. It's the week that I get to relive my early days and truly be myself.

And nobody knows the truth. Not Gordon. Not the Network. Not even my wife knew, rest her soul.

What's that? *Tell you about it*? No, I'm not going to tell you.

I'd have to kill you.

I am only joking. Perhaps.

But you seem nice enough. You've let me ramble on about nothing. And you've been generous enough to smile and nod and listen.

And that's important to someone like me. To have someone listen.

Really listen.

And I appreciate it. Really, I do. And if you've got nothing else to do tonight,

49

nowhere to go, then I hope you'll indulge me a for a while longer.

I have a lot to tell you. And quite a bit to show you along the way. Of course, I don't have any way of knowing what may happen with me tomorrow, or the next day, or the weeks and months after. But I do have the impression that someone is definitely out to get me.

And it would be nice to have someone with me. To help watch my back.

So what do you say? I'll even make you dinner.

I hope you like grilled ham and cheese. If not, that's all right. The wine will be exquisite. James Stewart will be outstanding.

And you never know when I may let something slip.

So get in the car. It's a Beemer, but we're in no hurry. This is Los Angeles. This city isn't going anywhere.

Just like me.

ENTRÉE

THE BLACK MARKET

Okay. I'll admit it. I can be pretty harsh on Los Angeles. I really do hate this fucking city, but it has it's admirable qualities.

The Midtown Farmers Market, for instance, is quite impressive. The Market itself came into existence during the Great Depression. Struggling farmers would bring their produce and goods to sell, trying to get by during those trying times.

Now, it's a very touristy destination. Souvenirs, knick knacks, and all manner of crap can be found in the seemingly endless line of tables and booths. But at it's heart the Market is still just that. A market.

I drop in rather frequently for fresh veggies, fish and exotic spices. There is an aging Greek couple who sell the most painfully delicious lamb souvlakia this side of the Atlantic.

I find myself at the Market today hoping to score some fresh Portobello mushrooms, radicchio, and a few links of spicy pepperoni. As usual, I get a few gawkers. I sign a few autographs, pose for a few pictures, point out some savory looking romaine lettuce to a young gay couple. I see local chefs browsing for inspiration. Very familiar territory to me.

I notice a large display of grapes and I reach to sample a dark muscadine. Then I hear the crash.

And then I hear the screams.

I watch as the table before me, with the baskets of grapes, flips over as a car, an old Lincoln Continental, glides through the Market. Tent poles snap. Baskets of carrots, buckets of crabs, bushels of unidentifiable fruits and vegetables, everything is flying everywhere.

A young man who had been standing beside me, was now tumbling from the air, his face crushed in from the impact with the speeding car.

The car hits a light pole and comes to a stop. The engine hissing, people crying and moaning. I am disoriented for a few moments. Within seconds police are surrounding the car, guns raised, calling out warnings and demands to the driver.

Finally, an old man climbs out of the car, crying. He looks to be in his late eighties or so. He is apologizing. He says that he had turned the wrong corner and hit the accelerator instead of his brakes.

The man looks pitiful. Shaken. Ashamed. The police lower their guns, and ambulances are called in.

Three people I can see are quite obviously dead. The young man with his face crushed in, and two teenage girls laying in the street. One of the girls, poor thing, her stomach was torn open. Blood and organs spilt out beside her.

I stare at her face. And I think of Abigail. My late wife. She was at the New York market the day she died. And then she was on that cold table.

I look away from the girl's face.

I see her intestines. I see what might be her spleen. I see a lot of blood. It's everywhere. And then it hits me. I wanted a beef liver to prepare for dinner. It would go quite well with the mushrooms. I think I'll skip the radicchio. Substitute some squash or eggplant.

Yes. Sounds delicious.

I look back at the girl's face. Poor thing.

She probably never even tried liver before.

THE DONOVAN RUSHING CHURCH
OF CULINARY SALVATION

When you spend as many years in this business as I have, you would think that you would become more than a little complacent. This is true for many people, as is the case in any lifelong career situation, but I have never become too comfortable in this field. I love it, sure. I love cooking, it's the core of my very soul, but for me there has always been that thin veneer coating a rolling boil of chaos that has kept me on my toes.

While technically I don't cook professionally very much at all anymore, even on my television show I am merely half-preparing everything, going through the basic motions as my staff does all of the real cooking for me offstage, I still consider myself a chef.

And I still have Rushing's.

I have seven restaurants throughout the United States, but Rushing's was my first and most successful. The restaurant opened for business in October of 1980, and to this day it is still one of the busiest in Manhattan. Originally conceived as a French and Mediterranean haute cuisine restaurant, it has grown over the years into something a little more street level and public-friendly.

While the same specialty dishes are still prepared in the massive kitchen, the presentation has changed to fit with the comfy atmosphere of the three hundred seat dining room (a Saturday night of six hundred and fifty covers is not unusual).

I am the executive chef, though I am only in the kitchen for two weeks every October, a sort of anniversary stint calling orders and getting into the heated bliss of it all. Many times I will work the pastry station, my first love. The head chef, Pascal Hernandez, is an absolute godsend, running the kitchen as I would, and when I am there with him I diligently take my orders along with the rest of the brigade.

But everyone knows who the boss really is.

I miss being there regularly. I haven't worked there full time since 1991. The eighties were the only time that I had the freedom of being my own boss, running a fantastic restaurant, living the life that I loved so much.

So many memories. Some good. Some not so good. Some downright stupefying. But that's how it goes in this world. It never changes. The faces change, yes. The names over the last decade or so have become more Mexican and Ecuadorian and Venezuelan, but the attitude, the mood of the restaurant kitchen in general, has been constant. Reliable. A martini in one hand and a bottle rocket in the other.

I remember one night in particular. It was a Wednesday I believe, sometime in the mid 1980s. A scraggly, smartass dishwasher we had hired about a month earlier was expressing his interest in moving up the brigade ladder. I don't recall his name. We went through so many dishwashers back then. Anyway, it was a little slow that night, so I agreed to let him work for the evening at the salad station. Melora, the vegetable chef, instructed him to go to the walk-in for a bag of lettuce. Now what she wanted was one of the bags of lettuce she had shredded earlier that day, but she was not this specific in her demand.

The young man spent several minutes in the large refrigerator, then finally emerged. Over his shoulder he was carrying a large bag filled with thirty heads of lettuce. Our supplier at the time delivered the lettuce that way. The young man was obviously having a difficult time carrying the monstrous bag, and everyone did their best to contain their laughter until the appropriate moment. He was almost back to the salad station when the bag split at the bottom and every head of lettuce spilled out and scattered around the kitchen floor.

This was the appropriate moment.

Everyone fell into hysterics. Our eyes filled with tears as our guts churned out rapturous laughter. The young man just stood there, frozen in his embarrassment.

When the laughter died down, he diligently picked up the lettuce and then retrieved the intended bag of shredded lettuce for Melora. Then, without a word, he walked out the door and it was the last we saw of him.

It was one of those reinforcing situations for me. Some people are meant for this life. Some are not. That nameless young man was clearly destined for something else.

One of the line cooks, Rafael DiNovi, volunteered to wash dishes for the night, and the next several nights, until we hired a replacement. Rafael is currently the sous chef at my other Manhattan restaurant, Il Pugno Di Cuoio.

This should illustrate my level of commitment to those who show commitment to me.

I have always paid competitive wages while maintaining an air of one hundred and fifty percent professionalism in the workplace. I try to hire only the best. Sometimes I make a mistake and hire the wrong the person. But these mistakes correct themselves sooner rather than later.

This is who I am. This is how I have been taught to be. I own seven restaurants not because I strive to control a massive culinary empire (which I am not ashamed to admit I have earned), but because I put so much time and energy into teaching these young cooks everything I know that when they exceed themselves and become true-to-form professionals, I desperately want to hold on to them. They could easily get outstanding jobs running someone's restaurant, i.e. one of the competitors, but why should they when I can offer to give them one of their own.

Rushing's and Il Pugno Di Cuoio in Manhattan. The Med in Boston. Rushing's South in St. Louis. The Grand Orchard in Portland, Oregon. Dreamlife in Miami. And El Colgado Caballo in Austin, Texas. All of my restaurants feature the best menus for their area, prepared by the finest brigades I can possibly assemble.

I am currently finalizing plans for Rushing's West here in Los Angeles, and an undisclosed operation for Las Vegas.

Eventually many more of the chefs and cooks employed by me will be ready to move on, and I'll find myself opening more restaurants, and more restaurants, and then even more.

I don't know how I'll be able to sustain it all. Gordon assures me that we can manage it, and I leave a good deal of the handling to him. Most of the time I am merely a figurehead. An icon. A name to associate with.

I get involved when I see fit, but I have so much going on at any given moment, and I'm not getting any younger, and I obviously have attracted secret saboteurs who seek to undermine my massive culinary empire. And on top of all this, I am living in Los Angeles.

Have I mentioned just how much I hate this fucking city?

Many people say I'm going crazy. And who's to say they're wrong? Certainly not me.

This life has a dramatic effect on

everyone who dives into it. They say if you can't take the heat, you should get out of the kitchen. Well, it's not the heat that will do you in. It's the cold outside. The normalcy of the real world. Boys kissing girls. Landlords with tempers. Mortgages. Credit scores. McDonald's. National Security alerts. Child molesters. Chronic entertainment addicts. Four dollar per gallon gasoline. Delayed flights. Missing knives. Shitty Hollywood remakes. Condescending public radio. Fascist talk radio. Tree huggers. Religious extremists. Couch potatoes. MTV without music. Hate crimes. Secret societies. Black helicopters. White limousines. Awards banquets. Thank yous. Apologies. Excuses. Regrets. Denials. Animosity.

These are the things that drive men crazy. The kitchen is really the only sane place I know. The only place I feel safe. As volatile and chaotic as it usually is, the kitchen is my church. The heat is my god. And I make my offerings in the form of lamb chops, seasoned sole, herb spattered dough, and swollen goose livers.

I make sacrifices of blood, shallots, butter and demi-glace. I sing the praises from the hymnals of Escoffier, Beard, Rombauer and Fischer. I have been baptized in sweat, grease and scalding water. I have bled, and returned again.

And I am but a man. I am Donovan Rushing. Cook. Chef. Restaurateur.

And more and more often, a tired old man.

Donovan Rushing. Dinosaur. Urban legend. Bones in the dust.

It's only a matter of time. I will die, tired and lonely. Or those who conspire against me will finally do me in. I don't know which I prefer.

What would you do in my situation? What more can I do that I haven't already done?

What's the point?

I need a drink. Or maybe twelve.

And then I need to sleep. For a month. Then I need to cook, until I exhaust myself again. But what's really going to happen is the same old shit. Day after day. Year after year.

This is the life I signed on for, I suppose. And I will take it like a man. And when I have a minute or two, to sit alone, in silence, I can reminisce.

About Sinatra. About friends. About disappointments. And about Abigail.

Don't worry, I'll tell you more about her in due time. Right now, I am feeling an intense longing to get out of town.

Yes. Los Angeles is weighing down upon me. I need to breathe. And the only place I know of where I could get to unwind is New York.

Home. Rushing's. Hundreds of fantastic restaurants. Dozens of exquisite bars.

Yes. This is what I need.

I pick up the phone. I make flight arrangements. And I pack a weekend bag. Socks. Underwear. Global knives. The essentials. I intend to have an incredibly relaxing, reinvigorating weekend.

And I can't think of anything that could possibly ruin this.

NEW YORK, NEW YORK

Brennen Moseley has been my personal pilot for the last seven years. He owns a beautiful Beechcraft King Air 300 that carries me around the country, wherever I need to go. While I'm not his only client, I am his priority client. And so if Brennen were to magically find himself in Michelle Pfeiffer's bedroom, with candles flickering and Percy Sledge on the stereo, and I were to call to inform him that I required a flight to the middle of Nebraska so I could camp out for a week and just take in the scenery, then he would drop what he was doing and fire up the plane.

Of course, I would never impose myself upon him in such a way, but sometimes I find myself really needing to get away for a few days. Like now.

I want to fly to New York City for the weekend. Visit the restaurants, check in on a few friends. I haven't been home since last October, and I feel I am long overdue.

I relax with a newspaper at the Haxan Aviation terminal for a half hour before Brennen arrives. In his mid thirties, with short cropped hair, muscular physique and perpetual five o'clock shadow, Brennen Moseley appears more apt to be a boxer or a cop from a 1950s detective film. He spends his off days cruising the coast on his custom Harley Fat Boy. But I can assure you that he is one of the nicest young men I've ever had the pleasure of knowing. And his command over his aircraft is impressive, even to other more seasoned pilots.

Normally when I travel I have my manager Gordon with me, along with my assistant and a few others. But this is a personal trip. After my breakdown at the studio a few days ago, I feel this is just what I need. To get out of Los Angeles. On my own. And besides, I still haven't been able to get in touch with Gordon, so I'm just assuming he didn't have something planned for me this weekend.

At a quarter to eight on this Friday morning, my stomach tightens a little as the King Air lifts into the air, leaving the runway far below. After about a minute the plane steadies, and I relax. We will fly from Los Angles to Dallas, and then to South Carolina, and finally make the final lap to New York, where we are scheduled to arrive around two local time.

The flight is smooth. Even with the stops, we make good time. The skies in the western hemisphere are mostly clear, and we encounter no delays. It's about time my luck turned back in my favor. I knew this trip would be a good idea.

I prefer to fly private because it is so much more hassle-free than going through one of the big corporate airlines or charters. Brennen is good company, keeping the mood light with just a little small talk. He's gotten to know me well, that I'd rather keep quiet than ramble on and on.

Which is why I suppose this is unusual for me. Here I am, sitting here, rambling on and on to you, and you are just taking it all in. You really are a good sport.

"You say something, Mr. Rushing?"

I look up to Brennen. Was I talking to myself again?

Peculiar.

"No, Brennen. I was just thinking out loud."

"Okay. You should know we'll be in New York in about twenty minutes."

"Thank you, Brennen."

On the seat next to me is a spiral-bound notebook. The most recent in hundreds I've accumulated over the years. Inside, I've scribbled and scrawled barely legible notes to myself, recipe outlines, shopping lists, phone numbers of new contacts, newspaper and magazine clippings, notes for the novel I've been writing (everyone is writing a novel these days), and various odds and ends of interest to me at any given moment. The books would be a nightmare for an orderly-minded person. No rhyme or reason to any of it. But it's the way I've always kept up

71

with anything. God help me if someone other than myself were to actually be required to find something in one of them. It would literally take them weeks.

When we touch down at the airfield just north of the city, we arrange for two chauffeured vehicles. Brennen will spend the weekend with friends, always a phone call away should I decide to cut my trip short.

I'll be spending the weekend busily running between a half dozen or so restaurants, including my own two, and a few clubs as well as my permanent apartment just a few blocks from Rushing's.

The apartment is my first stop in the city.

The complex maintains a reputation of exclusivity without the sort of pretensions you might find at a similar complex on the west coast. My apartment is a twenty-five hundred square foot architectural masterpiece. With high ceilings and tall windows, spacious rooms and completely customized kitchen. The kitchen at my house in Beverly Hills isn't nearly as nice as this one. Not by a long shot.

In the refrigerator I find bottled water, a few bottles of wine, and a McDonald's bag with a burger and fries. I hired a caretaker to come in once a week to look the apartment over for me. The fast food must be hers. Shame.

I use the bathroom (it was a long ride from the airfield) and then reach for the cordless phone. I dial the number that has been engraved on my heart for nearly three decades, and the phone at Rushing's begins to ring.

"Rushing's. This is Brittany."

Brittany? There was no Brittany last time I was there.

"Where is Sophia?" I ask.

"Sophia is on maternity leave," she says. "May I help you?"

"Is Carlos available?"

"Who is calling?" she asks. I hear other voices. Sounds busy tonight. Good.

"This is Donovan Rushing."

She goes quiet for a moment. Then "You mean *the* Donovan Rushing?"

"Yes," I say. "Did my voice not give me away?"

"Oh my god." I hear her say something inaudible to someone else.

"I would very much like to speak with Carlos," I tell her.

"Yes, sir. One moment."

I hear a click, and then dial tone. I sigh and roll my eyes. I wait a moment, and hit redial.

"Rushing's. This is Brittany."

"You hung up on me."

"Oh shit! I mean, dammit," she stutters a little. "I'm so sorry, Mr. Rushing. I wasn't expecting you to call."

"It's my restaurant. Why wouldn't I

call?"

"I don't know. They say you are usually busy."

"I am busy. And right now I would like to talk to Carlos."

"Yes, sir. One moment, please."

"And try not to hang up this time," I say.

"Yes, sir. I'm sorry."

I hear the click, this time no dial tone. A few seconds later the other end clicks again.

"Donnie Boy." Carlos' thick Brooklyn accent, with that hint of Spanish flavor, is always a welcome sound.

"Carlos. It sounds busy tonight."

"Yes," he says. "We're booked with almost seven hundred covers."

"My lord, Carlos. You'll be there until four in the morning."

"Maybe. But at least I'm not in the kitchen. I'm getting too old for that amount of work."

"Nonsense. You could outcook me any day of the week."

"True, but we are still too old."

We share a brief laugh, although inside I am repeating that. *We are still too old.* Not something I want to think about, but I can't help it.

"You're in town." He doesn't really ask. He just says it.

"Yeah," I say. "I want to get together. I need to clear my head for the weekend."

"Los Angeles getting the better of you again."

"Pretty much."

"Tomorrow night is good," he says. "I don't think the restaurant will collapse without me."

"Hey, that's the reason I hired you."

He laughs, but I am serious. I could not trust my restaurant in anyone else's hands, since I couldn't be in control any longer.

"Elizabeth is out of town," he tells me. "We'll have a boys' night out. Like old times."

"Like old times," I repeat. For a quick moment I think of a long gone time. The early 1970s. Carlos and Elizabeth. Abigail and I. My mind wants to linger, but I force it away.

It's not healthy to dwell on the past for too long.

"Six o'clock," I say.

He agrees and I let him get back to work. Tomorrow night will be for fun, but tonight is for work. For Carlos, anyway. For me, tonight will be for rest. It's been a long day. And my legs and back ache from the flight.

From the wine closet I pick out a nice

bottle of Riesling. I take the bottle to the couch. No glass, I'll just drink straight from the bottle. I wish I had some cheese. A little food snob's comfort food.

I turn on the television and hit the menu button on the satellite remote. I type James Stewart into the search box. *Take Her, She's Mine* comes on in about twenty minutes. Good timing. Although I'll probably be out cold in only ten.

I grab my iPod. I put on my headphones. I hit the button. Doris Day sings to me about that old feeling. I lean my head back and shut my eyes.

I take a drink. The wine is wonderful. I let my mind drift back to the seventies. To old times.

To Abigail. And I don't fight it. I linger.

I see her eyes. Green, with hints of yellow. I can smell her hair. Lavender, from flowing blonde waves. I can feel her. Her arms wrapped around me. Her lips to my cheek.

"I love you," she says.

I love you, too.

And she's gone. Like she was never there. I almost cry. But it's too late.

I'm out cold.

CAB FARE FOR THE
HOMELESS CHEF

At 10:30 AM, I am knocking at the rear entrance door at Il Pugno Di Cuoio, my Italian restaurant in Manhattan. I opened the restaurant in 1991, my first new venture since opening Rushing's a decade earlier. My television cooking show had gained a lot of popularity during the Eighties and I was constantly being approached by investors and potential partners for restaurant contracts. I had declined them all until Lucy Gayle came to see me.

Lucy had worked the sauté station at Rushing's for about five years until she left to accept a sous chef position at an Italian restaurant in Boston in '88. She had done very well for herself in just a few years there, and when she decided she wanted to open her own place, she came to seek my advice.

Lucy had secured just over half the money she would need when she came to see me. She wasn't looking to hit me up, she just wanted me to tell her that she was not making a mistake. I told her that every restaurant was a potential mistake. Rushing's had done well during it's first decade, but I had seen countless other restaurants open and close for one reason or another (or usually for several reasons compounded).

But Lucy was dedicated to her intentions. She enthusiastically showed me her meticulously detailed business plan, the floor plans for the proposed kitchen and dining room. She showed me her initial menu, all authentic Italian, heavy on the cheese, with very little red sauce to be found. I was astonished. I fell in love with her restaurant right away. I made her an offer, right then, without hesitation.

The truth is, I had been thinking of opening a new restaurant for some time. I had merely been waiting for the right concept to come along. In only fifteen minutes, without hardly trying, Lucy had completely sold me on her Italian dream.

We went in as equal partners, opening Il Pugno Di Cuoio in August. I acted as owner, and Lucy was the head chef. There was a restaurant manager, but most of the decisions were made by Lucy. And now, seventeen years later, Lucy is still running the place herself. She has earned three stars from the *Times*, published a few cookbooks, and recently turned down an offer from the Food Network.

She told me it was because it would take her away from what she loves. The restaurant. I told her I could empathize with her fully.

The door opens and there is a young Latino man, about eighteen or so, standing just inside.

"Meester Rushing," he says, a little surprised. "Can I help you?"

"I'm here for lunch," I say. "Is Lucy around?"

"Si. Come inside."

I go in and we walk down a small hallway that leads into the kitchen. It's not as big as the one at Rushing's, but it doesn't need to be. The dining room can only sit eighty-five at a time, and business has been a little slow lately. The restaurant is still making a profit, so things are fine.

"Donovan!" Lucy cries out as soon as I walk in.

We hug. She is almost in tears. This is why I like being in New York. People are happy to see me.

"How have you been," I ask her.

"You know. Same old fucking shit."

Potty mouth, same as always. And stunning to look at. If she weren't a lesbian I'm quite sure that Carlos would have tried to bed her. I wouldn't be surprised if he had tried anyway. And I wouldn't be surprised if he'd succeeded.

"Well, I am starving," I say. "What would the chef recommend for lunch?"

Several minutes later, Lucy and I are sitting at a small table in a back corner of the dining room drinking from a Pinot Grigio from the Alto Adige region of northern Italy. She has been telling me all about her partner, Josie, and how in love they are with each other.

"It's just," she says, pausing for a moment. "I know that she is my soul mate. You can just feel it, you know? You just know it."

"I know what you mean," I tell her. And I do. It was the way I felt with Abigail, so many years ago.

"We're going to be married," Lucy says, smiling.

"Well, I suppose that congratulations are in order."

"It will be a little while, of course. When the elections are over, and I am sure that Obama will win the White House, then the changes can begin. And it will be only a short time until we can do it legal and official like everyone else."

"I hope it will work out for you."

"It will." So confident, she is. About everything.

A runner emerges from the kitchen with my lunch. Lucy had told me to try the new special: garlic and herb-crusted pork with gorgonzola sauce and a side of steamed baby artichokes. The meal is spectacular, as can be expected from Lucy and her staff. Her restaurant is the only one I almost never have to worry about. Her only real competition is one of Mario Batali's restaurants, but really the food here is so unique and individual there's really no competition at all.

I thank Lucy and her cooks for a wonderful lunch, and I take to the streets. New York is really one of the only true living cities of the world. There is so much history. So many cultures blending together. So much to see and do. So much to experience.

Most native New Yorkers grow accustomed to the city. It's just the place they live. It's not unusual for a tourist to stop and ask a local how to get to the

Empire Stare Building, and the local really has no idea. They never gave a damn about the Empire State Building. But they can tell the tourist where to get some really wonderful spicy Vietnamese food in Queens.

I have never been the typical New Yorker. I have eaten the city up, figuratively and literally, every bar and alley, every high rise and tenement, every sidewalk and ship dock. I get so excited, I'm almost worse than a tourist. Of course, now I sort of am a tourist. I live in Lost Angeles. But it doesn't feel like home. My apartment here in New York is comfortable and familiar, but doesn't really feel like home either. I guess I am homeless, in a way. Rich, successful, and homeless. That is me. I take notice of a few homeless men gathered near a shelter entrance. I wonder how many restaurants they own. What their houses in Los Angeles are like.

I wave for a taxi, and tell the driver to take me to Queens. I give him an address, and we are off. I do this every time I visit New York. A short while later we pull up in front of a rundown two-story building on a poor street. I tell the driver to leave the meter running, and I step out of the cab. I walk up to the building and peer in though the old, cracked windows.

It's a real shame. This building used to be so nice. Now it is nearly falling in on itself. A perfect match for more than a few other buildings in this neighborhood. I can see the dust-caked counter where my father would take orders, and the long counter in the back where so much dough and batter was thrown together. I can almost smell the bread baking right now. Almost taste the juicy sweetness of my mother's blueberry muffins. My god. This rotten, derelict building still feels like home. Like I could just walk in, grab a bag of flour and get to work. But those days are long gone. Decades away from here and now.

There is a realtor sign in the window. It's been there for years, faded by the relentless sunlight. I called the number once, sometime in the eighties, but it was out of service. I don't think anybody owns the place anymore. I don't know if I would actually buy the building, if given the chance. What would I do with it? It would take so much money to fix it up, bring it up to code. And then the neighborhood isn't exactly bustling with economic prosperity. No. It's better this way. The past is past. You have to keep moving. Pushing on.

I linger for a few more minutes, then get back into the cab.

"You alright, buddy?" The driver asks.

"Yes. I think I'm fine," I say, wiping my eyes.

"Where to now?"

"Back to Manhattan," I tell him. "Rushing's restaurant on Park Avenue."

"You got a reservation," he asks. "I hear you gotta call like a coupla' months in advance."

I laugh to myself. "No. I don't have a reservation. But I think it will be okay."

"Suit yourself, pal."

The city seems to blur outside the window, even though it's impossible. We're going maybe fifteen miles an hour, probably less. But New York is just so vast. Out the window, it just keeps moving and moving. On and on. I laugh to myself again. I intend to get incredibly fucked up tonight. I'm sure that Carlos will see to it. I've been putting it off for a while, but I can't wait anymore.

Tonight, it will be whiskey and wine. Sake and rum. Alcohol is calling out for Donovan Rushing. And Donovan Rushing is calling out for her.

ONE NIGHT IN RUSHING'S

"Donovan Rushing, you are one seriously serious bastard!"

Carlos and I are walking up the sidewalk, having already tossed a few shots at Greene's Pub. I have been simply telling him, for the twelve hundredth time or so, my opinions on the obesity crisis in America today. It is, in my estimation, the fault of the American mindset. The idea of Americans having the illusion of the freedom to do what they want without serious repercussion. Not the fault of conglomerate fast food purveyors or of individuals with an "addiction" to sugars and trans fats.

"You sound so unpatriotic," Carlos tells me. "Even with a nice dose of vodka in your gut, you can't just loosen up. You're so god damn serious all the time. It's sickening."

"I can't help it Carlos. I'm afraid it is my nature."

"Is it your nature to be a communist?"

"No," I say. "I'm not criticizing the American ideal, I am happy to indulge like everyone else. I am just pointing out the facts as I see them."

"Well, I for one am in no mood for facts tonight."

"Next stop, old friend?"

"To the Circuit Club," Carlos says with drunken glee.

The Circuit Club. One of New York's oldest and still operating jazz-based nightclubs. One of our favorite places in the city. The perfect place for me to unwind. And thank God it's only four blocks away. In little time at all, we are approaching it's grey-bricked façade.

Inside, the Circuit Club is all shadows

91

and neon lights, reflecting off black glass tables and dark red leather couches. The place has seen better days, decades ago, but it is still like stepping back in time. It was Sinatra who turned me on to this place, in the seventies. Once I started coming here, I was hooked. Unfortunately, I haven't been able to come here in a couple years, and the clubs in L.A. just don't measure up. San Francisco has some decent clubs, but nothing like this.

A few years ago the place would have been filled with smoke, like a fog so thick you could barely make out the stage from the entrance. Now the air is so clear and clean, it's practically heartbreaking. What's a jazz club without that heavy nicotine haze clinging to everything. Stupid politics and city ordinances.

Carlos and I walk up to the bar and order a few drinks. Carlos gets a scotch on ice, I go with a basic martini. On the stage is a rough-looking baby grand piano, the club's own. It's old as hell, but restrung and tuned up a couple times a year. Everyone from Elton John to Harry Connick Jr. have sat at that piano, sometimes just on a whim while visiting the club, interrupting someone else's set.

Tonight, there is a young woman sitting at the piano, rummaging through a stack of papers, music and lyric sheets presumably. She is rather short, in her twenties, with bleached hair and auburn roots.

"She's cute," Carlos says into his scotch.

"You're old enough to be her father," I tell him.

"Grandfather," he adds.

I laugh. I can't help it. Carlos has always been the perpetual wolf, a true lady killer. Even in his sixties, he has refused to slow down. His affairs are innumerable, and I'm sure his libido will be the death of him. Remarkably, he has aged well, still looking fifty at the most, with just a little grey highlighting his jet black hair. It's got to be the Spanish genes, I've told him. Old horny bastard, I almost envy him.

The young lady at the piano turns on her microphone. "How is everybody tonight?"

A number of people in the room give a cluttered response, and it would seem that the majority of them are doing well.

"My name is Heather Christian," she says. "And these are my songs."

With that, she begins to play. Her fingers moving like a surgeon's over the keys of the piano. My curiosity is instantly piqued. When she begins to sing, I am blown away. Her tiny voice takes on an older, erratic quality. I think of black jazz singers of the forties and fifties. Sudden jumps in pitch and tone, but carefully progressive. Drastic time changes, but dark and mellow, I am in awe. And I realize, she reminds me of me. It's probably how I would sound if I could sing. She's brilliant. I have never seen or heard anything like her.

And I should point out that I am not a fan of checking out newer, younger musical acts. Over the years I have been tricked by line cooks and runners into accompanying them to see hot, avant-garde so-called musical performances by such acts as Sonic Youth or Sleepytime Gorilla Museum (my

God, the headache I struggled through after that one). There was a nice cello group called Rasputina I once saw, but even they were a little rough at times. When I can, I stick to the classics. Of course, I have enjoyed shows by Leonard Cohen, Diana Krall (what a talent she is), Rufus Wainwright and a few others, so you can see where my musical tastes lie. Just peek into my iPod.

One song after another, this bewitching Heather Christian sings and plays her very heart out. She seems to forget there is even an audience watching her at all. She is in her own world.

Carlos says he is going to talk to her after her performance. I just roll my eyes.

"I just want to meet her," he says. "No funny business. I swear."

"Sure…" I say.

When her last song is over, the young singer thanks the audience, and begins to put away her things. This is when Carlos springs into action.

He approaches the stage and gets her attention. I don't know what he is saying to her, but since she does not instantly slap him, I can only assume he is behaving like a gentleman or that she is one tough little cookie. After a moment he gestures towards me, and she looks my way. She smiles and nods to him, and he walks back to the bar.

"Well?" I ask.

"She's sweet," Carlos says. "She wants to meet you."

"Relying on your association with a celebrity to pick up girls," I say. "You should be ashamed."

He just laughs, orders another drink. A few minutes later the young songstress joins us at the bar.

"Mr. Rushing," she says. "It's an honor to meet you."

"The honor is all mine, my dear." I take her hand, kiss the back like a true gentleman. "Your performance tonight was enlightening."

"Thank you," she says, blushing.

"We are heading to Rushing's next," Carlos says. "Have you ever been?"

"No," she says. "I've always wanted to. I've heard great things."

"You are more than welcome to join us," Carlos says. "If you have no other plans."

"I would love to," she says. "If it is okay with Mr. Rushing."

"It's Donovan," I tell her. "And I insist you join us."

"Donovan," she says.

Carlos is practically drooling. Old dog.

We arrive at Rushing's at a quarter to nine. The restaurant is busy. It almost looks full, but I know there are a few tables left open just in case. It's always been a requirement at all of my restaurants.

We enter into the front foyer and are

quickly greeted by an unfamiliar girl.

"Good evening," she begins. "Do you have a reservation tonight?"

She looks at Carlos and starts to blush with embarrassment. "I'm sorry Carlos, I didn't notice you for a moment."

"That's okay, Brittany," Carlos says. "I'd like you to meet Heather Christian and Donovan Rushing."

Brittany looks at me and her jaw drops. "Oh. My. God."

She rushes over to take my hand. "Mr. Rushing, I want you to know what a great honor it is for me to work in your restaurant. The past few weeks have been the most fulfilling of my life."

"Thank you, my dear," I tell her. "Carlos tells me you are doing an exceptionally wonderful job."

She blushes even more, her eyes shooting towards Carlos, who seems to be nearly sweating. Dear lord, Carlos. Not her too.

"A three-top, if you don't mind," Carlos tells Brittany, quickly moving past her.

Moments later we are seated, surrounded by a sea of chattering foodies and upscalers. I am beginning to wish we had simply grabbed a few hot dogs and gone to the beach.

Carlos drowns himself with glasses of wine as Heather tells us more about herself. Born in New Orleans, and raised in Mississippi, she's had a lifelong love for music, art and poetry. Her desires brought her to New York where she has made a name for herself on the local independent music scene. Carlos and I are telling her we intend to purchase one of her CDs, I mention her songs would go well on my iPod, when something grabs my attention from the far side of the dining room.

My eyes must be fucking with me. It can't be.

But yes. It is.

My manager, Gordon Hessler, sitting

at a table with some hippie-looking fellow in sunglasses and a fedora hat. Gordon is all smiles, chatting up the hippie.

"Excuse me for a minute," I say, getting up from the table.

I walk across the dining room. As I approach their table, the hippie notices me first. He takes off his sunglasses, prompting Gordon to look towards me, surprised.

"Donovan!" He yells, smiling wide. "What are you doing here?"

"I was going to ask you the same thing."

"Well," he says, with a brief pause. "I'm sorry I have not returned your calls in a few days. I thought you could use a break from the whole businessman side of things."

"You thought right," I tell him. "Who's your, um, friend?"

"Oh yes! My manners. Donovan, this is Eddie Blake."

The hippie stands up and extends his

hand. "Mr. Rushing, it's great to meet you."
He is staring at me hard. The eye contact is
a little uncomfortable. He's wearing an aged
t-shirt that says Butthole Surfers on it.
Whatever the hell that means.

Eddie Blake. Eddie Blake. Why is
that name familiar?

"Eddies a chef, Donovan," Gordon
says, reading my mind. "Had a few shows
on the MTV."

"Of course, sure," I say. I now recall
having read a few articles about this
arrogant, rebellious, rock and roll hippie
chef.

"He's looking for a change of pace,"
Gordon continues. "So I just signed him on
as a client."

What the fuck?!

"Really?" I ask, hardly masking my
surprise.

"Mr. Hessler has told me about
everything he has accomplished for you,"
the hippie says to me. "He seems like a good

man to have on your side."

"Gordon is great," I tell him. "I wouldn't be here without him."

"Well, as much as I love hearing others praise me," Gordon says. "Eddie and I were about to leave."

"Have you eaten yet?" I ask.

"Yes," Gordon says. "I had the salmon, and Eddie went with the rack of lamb."

"It was delicious," the hippie adds.

"I didn't cook it," I retort. Careful, Donovan. "So.. Congratulations, Freddie."

"Eddie," the hippie corrects.

"Of course," I say. "Gordon." I nod to my manager, then head back to my table.

"I'll call you," he says, his German accent melting into the din of the room.

"Is that Gordon?" Carlos asks as I sit back down.

"Yeah."

"Who is that other guy?"

"Some hippie cook," I say. "Gordon's new client."

"New client?" Carlos asks, puzzled. "Since when does Gordon Hessler take on new clients?"

"I've just been wondering the same thing," I say, turning around to see Gordon and the hippie getting up to leave.

"That's Eddie Blake," Heather says. "I've seen him on TV. He had this show where he went around eating meals made with outlawed ingredients. He's pretty famous."

"Fame doesn't make one a good cook," I say. "I just don't know what Gordon plans to do with him."

After several minutes of uncomfortable silence, even Heather keeps mum, our food arrives. Heather has boiled crab legs with raw oysters, and steamed artichokes. Carlos has the rack of lamb with sautéed onions and potatoes. I go with a steak, since I've lost my appetite for anything in particular. Afterwards, Heather orders a dark chocolate sorbet, but Carlos and I skip desert.

Everyone has enjoyed their dinner, especially young Heather, who can not seem to stop praising the cooks. We call it a night, Heather heading towards Central Park to meet up with friends, and Carlos staying at the restaurant, presumably waiting for Brittany's shift to end. The man is a dog, I swear.

I catch a cab and head down 7th Street, for the East River, a place of refuge for me in my younger years, though from the Queens side back then. I find a bench at the park with an ignorable amount of crud caked all over it, and I sit down.

Behind me, I hear the city. Loud. Obnoxious. Alive. In front of me, the river. The waning moon high in the sky, reflects down upon the cool water, as if some one-eyed god, like Odin perhaps, were slowly winking down at me.

What the hell is the deal with Gordon? For nearly three decades that man has been my manager, not to mention producer and trusted friend. I have been his only client. He has turned down some pretty well known chefs over the years.

And so why now? Why suddenly decide to take on a new client? And why this hippie? Eddie Blake. What's so special about him? Long ratty hair, goatee, thrift shop fedora. I think he's in his forties, but he could pass for thirty easily. He's a pretty boy, too. Gordon hates pretty boys. He's always joked that's why he's stayed so committed to me.

Heh..

Why should I even care? It's Gordon's life, he can do what he wants. He rarely makes a wrong move, so I should trust him. I can only wish him luck with his new client.

Besides, it's just a hippie. Nothing to be afraid of.

I take out my iPod, and slip the headphones onto my ears. I press play. Perry

105

Como. "Little Man You've Had A Busy Day." I close my eyes. Yes, that's better. Just relax, Donovan. Just chill. Everything will be okay.

Like I said. It's just a hippie.

Nothing to be afraid of.

POISSON

THE ART OF PERSUASION
TO BUY ART

"I have something incredible to show you, Mr. Rushing."

Julius Moore has a deep, old English accent, although he looks to be in his twenties. For such a young man, he certainly knows a lot about art culture and history.

I enter his spacious loft-style apartment, and even though I am not particularly interested in art, I can not help but feel a little impressed by the collection he has amassed. Several times a year I meet with Julius to look though the paintings he has acquired in his travels. I generally buy a few pieces of art as investments, but sometimes I will see a painting that I actually like.

I follow Julius, with his brown ponytail and dark teal designer suit, to his office at the far end of the apartment.

"It is quieter in the office," he explains to me. "I have guests from New Orleans staying in the spare bedroom."

He goes to a corner in his office, and flips through a bundle of paintings leaning against the wall. After a moment, he finds what he is looking for and pulls out the dark canvas to show me.

"This is *The Whisperer In The Shadow Of The Mountain*. From Richard Upton Pickerman. 1924."

The painting is a dark forest landscape, with an ominous mountain in the distance. Storm clouds swirl around it, like grey tentacles of smoke in the sky. It's horrible.

"It's very nice," I say.

"Nice? Mr. Rushing, I don't think you understand the importance of this piece. It is one of Pickerman's most brilliant works. It

110

marked a major turning point in his style."

"How much did you pay for it?"

"One twenty."

"And how much do you hope to get for it?"

"Two."

"That's an awful lot for one painting, Julius."

"It's worth three at least," he says.

"How did you get it so cheap?"

"I persuaded the owner to cut me a deal," he says with a hint of a grin. There's almost something sinister about this young man. Or perhaps it's just my crazy brain messing with me, as everyone is fond of thinking.

"I don't know," I tell him. "I was hoping you'd have something else from Emile Nolde."

"His pieces are getting hard to come

by," he says.

"How about Georgia O'Keefe?"

"Don't insult me, Donovan. I deal in art, not crap."

"I just don't know if I want this painting. I don't really have the money for anymore art right now."

"I specifically had you in mind when I bought this piece," Julius says, with faint disappointment in his eyes. This is how it starts. His art dealer voodoo. I'll most likely be buying this painting, no matter how much I dislike it. I just can't seem to be able to refuse this young man.

The few times that I actually have been able to turn him down, I felt strangely guilty afterwards. And so I take another look at the painting.

"Julius," I say with a pause. "I absolutely hate this painting. I would rather bake my own eyes into cupcakes than purchase this painting."

Several minutes later, as I am carrying

the painting, wrapped in paper, out of the office, I see his guests. A woman and a younger girl, about fourteen. Mother and daughter I suppose. Although the woman seems too young. I nod to them on my way out. They nod back over cups of coffee. The woman looks very hungry. Staring at me.

From their looks, it would appear that they've hit some hard times. So Julius is helping them out. Pretty generous. Perhaps he is not so sinister after all.

The weight of the painting in my hand reminds me that Julius does have a strange, demanding presence. But then again, so do I. According to what I've read in the food snob journals. People call me Mr. Sinister. Eccentric. Unpredictable.

I don't see myself that way at all. I'm just a cook. Who buys art that he hates. What's so strange about that?

Tomorrow I return to the studio to begin filming the next wave of episodes for *The Main Course*. Three weeks to shoot fifteen shows. I'd cancel them all if I could. But I've been stalling more than enough.

It's high time for me to get back to work. Back in gear.

It's time to show everybody that Donovan Rushing is still running this circus. Donovan Rushing is still the decision man.

I only wish I could gather the nerve to put this two hundred thousand dollar painting in the trash on my way home. Instead, it will go into storage, or on one of the walls of my Beverly Hills home, where I will be able to see it everyday, and loathe it more and more, along with the rest of the crap I have to put up with.

But that's fine. Plenty of people have it worse than me. The majority of American citizens have it worse than me. But that doesn't change the fact that I'm dissatisfied.

Abigail would surely kill me for feeling this way. But I can't help it. I hate this city. I hate this business.

And god damn it if somebody fucks up on set tomorrow I swear I just might bake their eyes into little fucking cupcakes.

THE HIPPIE VISITS THE SET

I never realized before just how big the studio is. When there is nobody here. No faces in the audience seats. No little voices from the control room.

I have been standing at the workstation on the stage for about twenty minutes. All alone. Security let me in. Didn't even ask why I was here early. I've never been here like this. It's peaceful.

Relaxing.

"Donovan?"

I turn to see Dean Prescott, the show's director, coming in from the spare kitchen. He has an armload of folders and notebooks.

"Hello, Dean."

"What's going on," he asks. "Is something wrong?"

"No, I was just in the neighborhood."

"You didn't need to be here until another three hours from now."

"I know. I had nothing better to do," I say with a grin. "Do you need any help with anything?"

"No. Thanks. Just paperwork."

He starts to head towards the office in the rear of the studio, above the audience, but he stops and turns back to me.

"Oh, Donovan, I was going to wait until later, but since you're already here…"

"What is it," I ask him.

"When, uhm… Mr. Blake gets here… Where do you want him?"

"Excuse me?"

"Do you want him on your left, or your right? We may need to reposition the cameras."

"Eddie Blake?"

"Yeah. He's doing the guest spot…"

What the fuck? I have no idea what he is talking about. Why would that hippie, Eddie Blake, be doing a guest spot on my show? Without me knowing about it?

"Of course," I say, trying to not look foolish. "On my right, I suppose."

"Great. Thanks."

He heads up the steps to the control room. I slip out the side door, and retrieve the small cell phone from my pocket. I hit the menu button and scroll down the short list of names until I find Gordon's. I hit the tiny green send button.

"Donovan, good morning," Gordon says in his thick German accent.

"Gordon, where are you?"

"I'm on my way to the studio. You just waking up?"

"No. I'm at the studio."

"Already? Wow," Gordon says. "Didn't know you had an early bird in you."

"Gordon," I say, trying to stay calm. "Why is Eddie Blake coming to the show today?"

"Oh, don't worry, it's just a little guest spot," he tells me. "I'm just trying to get my new client a little exposure with a more serious audience."

"Why was I not consulted about this?"

"Yeah, sorry about that. This was sort of a last minute thing."

"Even still, Gordon. This is my show and you know I…"

"Chef Rushing," a voice behind me interrupts.

I turn my head. And there he is. The

hippie. Eddie Blake.

"I have to go, Gordon," I say into the phone before terminating the call.

The hippie extends his hand. As an involuntary reflex I extend my own for the handshake. My skin crawls as we shake.

"Mr. Rushing, I want to thank you for allowing me to join your show today."

"Yes," I say. My mind is a total blank. My only thought is that I am going to kill Gordon. Not really. But you know what I mean.

"I don't know if you'll even remember this," the hippie says. "I worked for you once."

"Really," I ask, a little dumbstruck. "When?"

The hippie starts to answer but he is interrupted by one of the producers who has stuck his head out.

"Mr. Blake," the producer says. "If you'll come with me I'll take you to wardrobe to get you fitted."

The hippie leaves with the producer, who hardly acknowledges me.

So. The hippie worked for me? I find that hard to believe. You'd think I'd remember something like that. But then again, my restaurants have had some brutal employee turnaround over the years. He could have slipped in under my radar, as a runner or a waiter I suppose.

Small world.

The next few hours are spent going over the show's recipe outline with the assistant director, Shannon Mizelle.

"We are shooting three shows today," I say. "Which one is the hippie... I mean, uhm, which one will Mr. Blake be participating in?"

"All three," she says.

"I thought it was just a guest spot."

"What I've been told," she says, "Mr. Blake will assist you all day, and then we'll make a decision about tomorrow."

"Tomorrow?" *What the fuck*?! "You mean he may be here tomorrow?"

"Didn't Gordon speak with you about this?"

The silence, and the unpleasant look on my face, is answer enough. Shannon nods her head, and slips out of the room.

God dammit, Gordon. What the hell are you up to?

"Five minutes, Mr. Rushing!" an assistant calls out from somewhere. I take a deep breath. Exhale slowly. I watch the crew. I listen to the audience filling the seats. And I wait for my cue.

And then, like clockwork, I hear the little voice in my ear. Counting down from five.

Four.

Three.

Two.

One.

And I take to the stage.

Hello, everyone. I'm Donovan Rushing. Welcome to The Main Course*!*

A quick swell of applause, like always. I read the teleprompter.

Today, I have a very special guest in the studio with me. You may have seen his extreme cuisine specials on MTV and The Travel Channel, but today he'll be assisting me with a hearty meal. Please, everyone, welcome chef Eddie Blake.

I gesture to my left, as the prompter instructs, but the hippie enters from my right. Someone is fucking with me already. Just keep your cool, Donovan. Stay professional.

"You're doing great, Donovan," the director's little voice says in my ear.

The hippie comes up to me and we shake hands for the camera.

Eddie, it's a pleasure to have you here today.

"The pleasure is and the honor is mine, Chef Rushing. What are we making today?"

Straight to the point, I like this guy!

The audience laughs. I'm not trying to be funny. I'm just doing what the teleprompter or the little voice in my ear says.

Today we are preparing a simple yet delicious Korean dish. Bulgogi salmon with bok choy and garlic mushrooms.

The audience moans with delight.

"Bulgogi salmon," the hippie says. "What exactly is that?"

Well, in Korea, bulgogi is a beef sirloin strip that has been marinated in a traditional soy sauce, along with sesame oil and local herbs and spices. For this preparation, I am simply replacing the beef steak with salmon.

"Sounds delicious," the hippie says.

Just wait until you taste it.

Aside from my discomfort over the situation, things go rather smoothly. The salmon is dished without a problem. I fake amusement at Eddie's jokes fed to him from the producers and writers. He does the same for me. We really seem to be getting along.

The entire time, I am trying not to linger on thoughts of killing him. Just slaughtering him in front of this audience.

We finish the first show, and move flawlessly into the second. The dish, braised rabbit with cider rice. Once again, no problems. No missing knives. No wrong ingredients. We never even have to make use of the spare kitchen.

But it's the third and final show of the day where things start to go a little off. As the hippie is taking a pork roast with Mediterranean rub from the oven, a woman in the audience stands up.

"Chef Eddie, I love you!"

The hippie smiles towards her, and

subsequently drops the pan, which hits the counter, splashing it's spicy liquids everywhere. Some of the harsh juice hits my eye, and I can hear my patience snap deep within my brain.

SWEET JESUS FUCKING CHRIST!

The audience laughs. What the fuck?

Fuck you, this shit hurts!

"Donovan, calm down," the little voice says in my ear. Production assistants rush towards me with water bottles, eye drops and towels.

Get that shit away from me!

"Chef Rushing, I'm so sorry," the hippie says.

Go fuck yourself, kid.

I storm out of the studio, a paper towel on my eye. I go straight for my car. I can still hear the director's voice telling me to get a grip and come back inside. I throw the earpiece from the window of my car as the tires squeal out of the parking lot.

My cell phone rings. I look at the little screen. Gordon Hessler. Out the fucking window.

"Fuck you all," I say to no one. Everyone.

There is a bar I'm friendly with nearby. I don't go very often, but it's really the only one in L.A. that I can enjoy going to. I arrive within minutes. Inside, I take a seat at the bar.

"Mr. Rushing, how are you today?" the bartender, Colt, says. I think he is a homosexual.

"I feel like shit," I say to him. "I need a drink to match."

"Yes, sir."

Two hours and a couple dozen boilermakers later, I am in a beautiful stupor. Chatting up a real estate agent on my left, while signing an autograph for a young lady on my right.

An hour after this, I am in a different

bar. Buying beers for anyone who can sing along to the Frank Sinatra song I choose on the jukebox. The song, "Star."

At yet another bar, I'm downing Bloody Maries while a comedian named Luke Oddman bombs on the open mic stage. He is so bad, I could almost cry for him. Poor bastard.

After this, a total blur. I haven't felt such bliss in a long time. My brain almost thinks I am in New York. Old New York. With the filth and the scum and noise and the jumble wobbly maker fuckers. HA HA!

Oh, skip the shit, beat man. I'm not as fucked as you.

Son of a bitch. Now I'm seeing things.

HA HAHAHAHA HA HA HAHAHA HA!

LOOK! The hippie. Eddie Blake. The hippie fucking hippie is fucking coming right at me. Ha Ha!

HA!

127

And it all goes black. And quiet. And calm. Thank fucking God.

And then I feel it. That warm, then hot, acid from the stomach, bubbling up through my throat. I throw my eyes open, sit up and spew the night's misadventures into a tall plastic garbage can.

And it just keeps coming. Just keeps spewing. Until I am dry heaving. Retching. Sobbing. Grasping for breath, I collapse back down. I close my eyes. I'm sorry, Abigail. I'm so sorry.

"This is a really nice couch," I hear myself say.

"Are you going to be alright?"

I open my eyes. I look around. The hippie is sitting in a recliner across from me.

Where the fuck am I?

"Where am I?"

"My apartment," the hippie says. "I didn't know where you live, and I had to get you from out in the open before someone started taking photos."

I look around the room. The apartment looks small. Probably two bedrooms. One bath. The kitchen is certainly a sad, tiny, disproportioned space.

"You were pretty fucked," the hippie continues. "It took me hours to find you."

"Well," I say, getting up. "I should probably get home." As I stand up, the room sways, my brain swims around in my head like cracked eggs in boiling water. I collapse back down to the couch, sitting upright at least.

"What time is it?"

"It's just after three," the hippie answers.

"Do you have some water?"

"I have some bottled," he says. "But it's not cold."

"No ice?"

"No. Sorry."

"That's fine," I say. I just need liquid.

The hippie gets up and leaves the room. I look around again. He's still just moving in, from the looks of things. Boxes stacked against every wall. Some labeled *records*. Some *books*. Others say everything from *paints* and *cars* to *taxes* and *scrapbooks*.

Only one picture has been hung upon the wall. A large black and white photograph of the hippie and writer Hunter S. Thompson, who I recognize from a social dinner I participated in during the late Eighties. On the long, dark coffee table beside me sits a dog-eared paperback book titled *The Devil's Lodge: The Louisiana Hunters Cult and Other True Mysteries* by Collin Monroe.

The hippie returns, handing me the bottle of room temperature distilled water. I twist off the cap and suck down nearly half the bottle.

"Thank you," I say.

"Sure. So, um… You sort of lost it a little bit, huh?"

"I suppose," I say. "I've been doing that a lot lately, I think."

"What's the deal? Stress or something?"

"No," I say. "I'm just realizing how little control I have over my own life. I don't normally drink like that. Not for a while now."

"I don't remember ever seeing you drink at Rushing's."

"At Rushing's?"

"Yeah," the hippie says. "When I worked there. Early Eighties."

"Oh yeah. I'm sorry, but I don't remember that."

"I was a dishwasher," the hippie explains. "The line cooks were always giving me a hard time. I was given a shot to move up, but I screwed up."

"What happened?"

"Well, I was helping the garde manger, and she sent me to the walk in for lettuce. She was wanting one bag, intending for me to get one of those five pound bags of chopped lettuce. Instead, I grabbed one of the bags with forty heads of lettuce by mistake."

I laugh a little. "You spilled the entire bag," I say.

"The lettuce rolled everywhere," the hippie adds.

"That's not much of a screw up," I tell him. My head is pounding.

"Yeah, but it was a number of things. My girlfriend had just dumped me, I was being evicted. And some other pretty serious shit. I was frustrated, so I quit."

"Well, it looks like things worked out for you."

"Yeah…"

There is a long, uncomfortable

silence. Neither of us are entirely sure what to say to each other. Christ, my head is really hurting. After several minutes, the hippie finally breaks the silence.

"You didn't really want me on the show today, did you?"

"No," I say, bluntly.

"I can't blame you," he says. "I have a pretty tarnished reputation."

"I really don't know anything about your reputation," I tell him. "I just don't like decisions like that being made without me."

"I'm sorry."

"Not your fault."

More silence. I break it this time.

"Look. We can talk about this shit tomorrow. When my head is a little more clear."

"Okay," the hippie says. "There is a pillow and blanket on the floor beside you. I'll leave the trash can."

"Thanks."

"You can watch TV, it won't bother me," he says, placing the TV remote on the coffee table beside me before leaving the room.

I grab the pillow, but leave the blanket. I take the remote and hit the power button and browse through a few channels. On one channel Time Life is trying to sell a CD collection of disco classics. On another, Wolfgang Puck is showing his audience how to make carrot and ginger soup. I gave him that recipe.

On another channel, a light-skinned black girl is sucking on the huge cock of an overweight white guy while pleasuring herself with a massive neon green vibrator.

Good. Fucking. God.

I hit the menu button and search. Satellite radio. I find the classic jazz station. I hit select.

The Louis Armstrong All Stars. "St. Louis Blues."

I set down the remote and close my eyes. My head is throbbing, my throat is sore, and my stomach aches. I can smell the pungent vomit in the garbage can nearby.

I am Donovan Rushing. Cook. Restaurateur. Television star. Human fuckup.

I am falling asleep on the couch of the hippie chef, Eddie Blake.

I am falling asleep in misery and shame. I am falling asleep with the music of Louis Armstrong in the air.

I am falling asleep…

I am falling asleep…

I am falling.

DREAM A LITTLE DREAM

Have you ever been so in love with someone, that when they were near you, it pained you to breathe? You want to just say something, anything, the right thing, that will make them smile, take notice of you. Understand you.

And hold you. Indefinitely.

Everyone, at least once in their lives, should find themselves in this precarious predicament. For me, it was so long ago, but it still feels like yesterday.

The very moment that I laid eyes on Abigail Preponi, I knew wholeheartedly, without a shred of a doubt, that I loved her. I didn't know anything about her, but I understood her instantly.

Naturally, it always takes the other person a little longer to come around to your way of thinking. But it is always worth the effort.

It was 1970. I was barely twenty seven. After running the kitchen at Dans La Merde for about four years, I was offered the head chef position at La Tabouret Courant, a very swank and prestigious French restaurant. Abigail was a waitress. She was eighteen. It took me two full weeks to say something to her besides "Table fourteen!" or "I need two more minutes on this foie!" I approached her at the neighboring bar after service one night, and we just hit it off. I fell for her. Hard.

We were dating by the next week. And engaged by the end of the year. I don't really know how to explain it to you. The impression she made upon me. Here she was, this beautiful, intelligent young woman, with the eyes of a long lost silent era movie star and a smile that could stop the devil himself in his tracks. And she accepted me, a strange, lanky, funny talking cook. She said that we were absolute equals.

I was a little older, sure. But I'd never really been in a relationship up to that time. I wasn't a virgin by any means. Being a cook in New York, a slave to the night, came with it's fair share of perks. I had just never met anyone that I connected with. Not like this.

Abigail loved jazz, and Sinatra, and was pretty familiar with James Stewart movies. She loved spinach. She hated spiders. And she had the tough take-no-shit attitude of a real New Yorker, even though she was from fucking Jersey.

When Abigail and I married the following spring, I felt whole. Complete. I was building a reputation as one of New York's premiere chefs. I had a beautiful and caring wife, and things just couldn't be better.

It was so strange, the wedding. Frank Sinatra came, and filled in for the priest. We had a beautiful wedding cake that I had baked myself. We had nearly a thousand swans, flocks of them throughout Central Park, where the ceremony was held. Funny though, the swans. They sort of look like vultures.

And why is no one smiling? And where is Abigail?

Why is Frank Sinatra dressed as a priest? That's not right.

What the hell is going on?

Someone, it looks like James Stewart, is cutting the cake. He is dressed like a cowboy. He has blood on his chin, pouring from his mouth. Blood pours from the cake as the knife slips through. It just flows.

Blood pours from the mouths of everyone in sight. And from the vultures' eyes.

A mafia boss approaches me, invites me to his private estate for a week. He has blood on his chin. Where is Abigail?

My parents congratulate me. My father says that he is so proud. He has blood on his chin. So does my mother. Where is Abigail?

Gordon Hessler comes up, says he has a marvelous idea for a new cooking show. I should sign a deal with him. He has blood on his chin. That's not right. I didn't meet Gordon until the next fall.

Where is Abigail?

Then I see her. Abigail. Laying on the ground, in a pool of blood. She's been shot four times in the chest. I try to go to her, but I can't. There is too much blood. I am just running in place, slipping and sliding in it.

"Order up!" someone yells.

"Order up!" another screams.

And then everyone. "Order up! Order up!" A thousand voices. Chanting. Taunting.

"Order up! Order up!"

Abigail. I'm sorry. Please wake up.

Please.

Wake up.

HANGOVERS (SUNNY SIDE UP)

Oh fucking hell. Where am I?

I strain to open my eyes, heavy morning sunlight pouring in through the windows. I am on a couch. I can smell vomit somewhere nearby. There is a large flat screen TV, autotuned to what appears to be some Michael Keaton movie, something from the eighties.

I look around the room, and I see a single framed photograph hanging on a wall. In the photo is writer Hunter S. Thompson and the rebellious hippie chef Eddie Blake.

Son of a bitch. Now I remember. I sit up, my back aching.

I listen for sounds of a hippie moving about, but the apartment is silent, save for the TV. I feel for my keys and wallet, undisturbed in my pockets, and I slip out of the apartment, making my way down to the street.

Fucking Los Angeles. It is eight in the morning and there are people everywhere. Sure, not that much different from New York. But it is different.

It smells different. It feels different.

I am hung-over. I am starving. I am lucky that I actually recognize where I am. A few blocks north should get me to Santa Monica Boulevard.

And I can get some breakfast.

I end up in front of Patchookum's Diner. I've never heard of this place. I guess it will suffice.

I take a seat inside, and order a coffee. Black. I glance at the menu. Mostly the basics, which is fine. I order a cheese and onion omelet, with a side of toast and sausage.

142

I stare down at my omelet. I feel a psychic connection with the chicken that the egg would have grown up to be.

"I forgive you," the baby chicken ghost says to me from the afterlife.

I reach for my cell phone to check my messages, only to remember I tossed it out my car window yesterday. I hope no one finds it. There are a ton of confidential numbers in that thing.

"Excuse me," a woman's voice to my left. "Aren't you Donovan Rushing?"

I turn to the woman, whom I vaguely recognize as an actress. I'm not sure which one. Actors look so normal in person, it's hard to pinpoint them sometimes.

"Yes," I say to her. "How are you?"

"I'm great," she says, smiling wide. "Would I be intruding if I asked for an autograph?"

"Not at all," I say, trying my best not to look intruded upon. My head is pounding

143

like a jungle drum and the coffee is barely masking the bile flavor in the back of my throat.

The young actress hands me a pen and a note card.

"And whom shall I make this out to?"

She smiles even wider and says "Alicia."

The name doesn't help me to identify her. I sign the card, and she thanks me before leaving. I wonder if she felt bad that I did not really recognize her.

As my food arrives, I realize that I don't sign that many autographs in Los Angeles. In New York, I actually grew accustomed to carrying a pen with me, because several people would always stop me, regardless of where I was going. People would just happen to be carrying my book, and they would nervously approach me. A few times I would hand out free meal cards to couples, good for any weekday evening at Rushing's.

Occasionally, someone will confuse

me with Anthony Bourdain, which I have never really understood. If I should run into him sometime I should ask if it ever happens to him.

I finish my breakfast, tip well, as always, and hit the sidewalk again. I wave down a cab and get a ride to The Gold Watch, the first bar I hit yesterday.

As I thought, my car is still in the parking lot. Untowed, untouched.

I get in the car, and start the mostly short trip home. As I am driving I notice that cars are blowing their horns at me for no apparent reason. After a few minutes, I am starting to get really pissed off. I am too hung-over for this bullshit. I pull in the driveway, and make a mental note to call the gardener, as the hedges are getting a little messy. I walk around the back of my car, and I see something. A bumper sticker. It reads: *Honk If You Love Motörhead!*

Jesus Mother Fucking Christ On A Crutch. What the fuck is up with this fucking shit?! Who keeps vandalizing my fucking car?! And what the fuck is a Motörhead?! I tear the sticker away, and storm into my house.

Inside the house, I turn on the TV, tuned to CNN. A chubby reporter is interviewing some Asian kid who seems to have built a working model replica of that giant airplane that Howard Hughes designed. The Loose Goose or whatever it was called.

Not much news to report apparently. I go into the kitchen and put a fresh pot of coffee on. I see there is one message on the answering machine. I hit the red button to play the message.

Donovan, it's Gordon. I don't know where you are, but when you get this I need you to call me. We need to talk. You know what this is about.

God. Damn. It.

When Gordon sounds like this, he's serious. He sounds like the Gordon from the early days. Dominant. Authoritative.

He sounds like a fucking SS henchman when he is like this.

It's the Gordon I haven't heard in a while.

Then again, perhaps now is my chance to make a stand. Speak my mind. Get all of this frustration off of my chest.

Yes. It is time for some changes. When Gordon hears me out, he'll understand.

I take a deep breath and pick up the cordless phone. This will be the first day of a new Donovan Rushing. Things will be going my way now.

Donovan Rushing will now be calling the shots.

DONOVAN RUSHING IS NOT CALLING THE SHOTS

Gordon Hesler's office is cold. Sterile. Like a dentist's.

It is odd, because his office is in his house, which is otherwise warm and inviting. Which is odd in itself, considering that Gordon lives alone. He has had girlfriends in the past, but he never committed to any of them.

"I can not allow anything to distract my attention from you," he has told me. And it is true. Gordon has taken care of me, and lived vicariously through me, but he says it was his fate. And I admit that I could have never accomplished this kind of success without his guiding mind. Sometimes I could swear the man knows me better than I

148

know myself.

Gordon sits at his desk, just staring at me for a while. He is wearing his running suit. He'll be going for his jog after this, so hopefully this won't take long. He loves to fucking run.

"Donovan," he finally says. "I am very concerned about you."

"Well you shouldn't be, Gordon."

"Your behavior yesterday, and over the past weeks…"

"I can explain that," I tell him.

"No," he says, a grimace on his face. "No explaining. No excuses. It needs to stop. The producers are worried, getting nervous. The Network is shitting all over their chairs."

I try not to smile. When Gordon is angry, his English gets a little hammered. But I can see that he is serious, so I restrain myself.

"They want to know that you are

okay. In your head."

"Really?" I ask. "They think I'm crazy?"

"They just want to be reassured. If you need some time off or something."

"I just had a vacation," I say.

"Not your fucking mystery week. A real break."

"No, Gordon," I say, sitting up straight in my seat. This is it. "I just need a few changes."

"What sort of changes?"

"Well," I say, full of confidence. "For starters, I am tired of decisions being made without me. I don't mind having guests on the show, but I like to know about it before the day of production."

"That's fair," Gordon says. "And I am sorry about that. But you should know that many decisions are made without me as well. I have to go along with the Network."

"I know that."

"Yes, and I need to make it very clear for you that Eddie Blake is no longer a guest on the show."

"I am glad to hear that."

"He is joining the show."

"Excuse me?" *WHAT THE FUCK*?!

"Your ratings have been down for over a year now. I could not hold the producers off any longer. They want a fresh face to help support you."

"Eddie Blake is joining the show?"

"Yes."

"The fucking hippie? Who wouldn't know real food if James Beard prepared and served it to him personally, is joining my show?"

"They said you can think of him as your sous chef."

"No fucking way, Gordon!"

151

"The decision has been made."

"I will not go along with this," I tell him. "I have worked too hard for too long to just hand my show over like this."

"It is not your show, Donovan."

"The hell it's not!"

"The contracts have always been in my name. It is my show, has been since the first day."

He's right. It's easy to forget. Gordon has always been the brains behind the operation. I was so young when we started this, and he was so trustable. My fate has been in his hands.

"There is nothing that can be done," he tells me. "This is the way it is. Your ratings will increase, a younger demographic will be earned for the show, and the show will live on."

"Why was I not consulted, Gordon?"

"The producers are tiny gods,

Donovan. They do what they want. If you don't like it, you can leave."

"Leave the show? Is that what they want?"

"Is that what you want?"

"No," I say. "Of course, not. I just.."

"I know this is a lot to take in."

"Yeah.."

"Take a week to get yourself straight," he says. "No drinking, get some rest. And look through this."

Gordon hands me a box.

"What is this?" I ask.

"It is homework."

I open the box. Inside are some books and a few DVD collections. All Eddie Blake material. His books. His TV shows. Research, I suppose. Fucking great.

Now I've got some fucking

homework to do. What is this, grade school for aging celebrity chefs?

"Get to know this man," Gordon says. "He's not so bad."

"Are you sure you want to do this," I ask. I think I may be going into shock.

"I have never been more sure of anything, Donovan. This is the way it has to be."

I sit for a moment, just staring down at the box of crap. This has not gone well at all.

"I have to do my jogging now," Gordon says, getting up from his chair. "There is a new cell phone in the box. Same number. It is all set up for you."

"Thanks.."

"Get some rest, please. I will call you in a few days."

I get up. I walk outside, carrying the box of hippie crap to my car. I get in the car. I turn on the radio. Satellite radio. I go to a preset classic jazz station.

Frank Sinatra. "My Way." Not quite, old friend.

Not even close.

LE COURS AIGRE

A BRIEF HISTORY OF THE
UNIVERSE OF THE HIPPIE CHEF
EDDIE BLAKE

Eddie Blake is from Kentucky. Strange. I'd have never imagined that. He was born in 1963. Probably raised by hippies.

I've been going through the box, my homework, that Gordon forced upon me. I watched one of the DVD collections of the late 1990s MTV show *Eddie Blake Can Cook Your Ass*. The box actually says *Kick Your Ass*, but *Kick* is slashed out with *Cook* superimposed. That's almost clever. Most likely the product of some producer's brainstorm.

I just started reading Blake's autobiography, *Sex, Drugs and Rockin' Food*, from 2007. I'm a few chapters in, and

I quickly reaffirm my loathing of this shaggy haired cook.

He had a rock band during his teens, Children With Guns, and they moved to California in search of their big break. Instead, Eddie was talked into taking an acting job. He appeared in a 1984 horror film, *Night-Terrors On Shadow Lane*. It was a flop. A disaster. It was his only film.

The VHS tapes of the movie are now collector's items. A big Hollywood remake is being planned for next year.

After this, he moved to New York. He doesn't mention in the book, but I look over his resume and find that he did indeed work five months at Rushing's in 1985. After he quit, he went to wash dishes at Debrouillard's. I never liked that place. Shitty faux-French crap.

In 1986, Eddie enrolled at the Culinary Institute, and dropped out after six months to accept the sous chef job at Vilain Plat. I remember that place. It was only open for a few years. The food wasn't bad. He became head chef in 1987. Means I ate his food a few times.

160

In 1989, he took the head chef position at Enfant Terrible, which is a dark hippie nightclub restaurant in Hell's Kitchen. I've never been there. They cater to the young celebrity and artist crowd.

This is where the hippie starts to go crazy. He is branded a womanizer and a crook. An all around troublemaker. Getting arrested, making the paper for his fights. Some of this shit is actually familiar to me now. I remember some of this.

Although, honestly, the same can be said of most chefs. I wasn't very squeaky clean myself early on. I still engage in some questionable activities. The things I have seen on my annual secret vacations... Dear god.

In the late 1990s, Eddie Blake becomes a TV chef. He starts as a cooking guest on the then-popular *The Tom Green Show*. He uses the publicity he earns from this to make a deal for his own show, *Eddie Blake Can Cook Your Ass*. The *Cook Your Ass* show lasts for two seasons, and in 2000 he becomes the host of *Late Night Snack*, a sort of Letterman-style show where he cooks with his guests. It becomes a sort of cult hit.

This show lasts until 2005, when Eddie moves over to the Travel Channel for his new show *Eddie Blake's Illegal Cuisine*, where he travels the world cooking meals made from endangered species, or using local decriminalized drugs in the ingredients. Only ten episodes were produced, but no one watched.

I can't say I blame them.

In 2007, Eddie takes part in Food Network's *Chef Of Steel* competition series. He wins the grand title at the end of the season. He is guaranteed a new cooking show on the network. I guess joining my show is the network's way of making good on that promise.

Winning the Chef Of Steel title is pretty much where the book ends. I've learned a lot, but still know nothing about this hippie cook. Why, in his book, did he leave out his time at Rushing's? He has made a lot of money over the years, but yet shows no real sign of spending it in someway. Never opening his own restaurant, or buying nice cars.

The man is just strange. An enigma.

Tomorrow I return to the studio. This hippie will be there. Gordon will be there. The network bigwigs will be there. They will be watching me. Judging me.

I am not looking forward to this.

It is out of my hands. But I can do this. I can grin and bear it. Stay calm. Stay professional.

Sooner or later, Eddie Blake will fuck up. And he'll be off the show, and then I'll have everyone where I want them. And I'll make them beg like dogs to their master.

And maybe, just maybe, I will spare them a fucking bone.

THIS IS NOT DONOVAN RUSHING'S ADORING PUBLIC

This has to be the second most uncomfortable day of my life. The first being the night I returned to work after Abigail's death.

I am standing on the stage at the studio. The usual plethora of producers, handlers, assistants, crew and hangers-on are scrambling about as always. The studio audience is full, to capacity, which would be normal except for the noticeable abundance of Eddie Blake t-shirts staring out from the small sea of foodies. I have never seen Donovan Rushing t-shirts in the audience. I don't even know if Donovan Rushing t-shirts exist.

Probably not.

164

The hippie, Eddie Blake, is standing at the cooking station, going over notes with a producer and a director. They don't even acknowledge me as I walk by, on my way to the spare kitchen offstage.

Angela, one of the production cooks, is chopping banana peppers, to apparently mix with a bowl of chopped garlic.

"Good morning, Angela"

"Chef Rushing," she says, setting the knife down.

"I hate to interrupt, my dear," I say to her. "But would it be too much for me to ask what we are preparing today?"

"Stuffed and grilled chicken breast fillets," she says.

"I suppose it was Mr. Blake's idea," I say.

"I believe so."

I look down at the peppers, very finely chopped. Perfect.

"Didn't you tell me once that you have no restaurant experience?"

"That's right," she says. "When I finished culinary school I got a job on a cooking show, and then another, and another. I've been doing this for fifteen years."

"And you've never had to deal with any of that professional kitchen bullshit."

"Nope."

"Clever girl, Angela."

And I mean it. She is paid well, doesn't have to worry about demanding patrons and snobbish waiters. She has the egotistic chef to contend with of course, but it is so much more relaxed in this setting. There's more time to devote to a dish. You're not rushing to get it done, you're concentrating to get it right. For the camera. For all of them, all of you, out there.

I head back out to the stage. An assistant wires me up with the little voice for my ear, a young woman checks my hair.

166

After all of the checks and balances of production preparation, I leave the stage to await the cue for my official entrance.

Eddie Blake is waiting as well.

"Chef Rushing," he says, approaching me.

"Mr. Blake," I say. "Nervous?"

"Not really. I've done all this before. I just hope that I don't disappoint you."

I don't think that anything could disappoint me ever again. My life is a boiling pot of piss and shit, and no matter how much seasoning I add to it, it will always be just piss and shit.

"You'll do fine," I say. "Just follow my lead."

I hardly look at him.

The day's production goes rather well. I bite my tongue, hit my marks, do all the shit the producers want. I try my best to show that I'm all right. That I'm not crazy.

I can't lose my show. I just can't.

As production wraps later in the day, three shows in the can, Eddie Blake is signing autographs for people in the audience. Greasy young men and women who look like rejects from a Marilyn Manson concert.

Marilyn Manson. I can hardly believe I know who that is. I think he was on one of the hippie's TV shows a couple times. Cooked some sort of lamb dish with absinthe, if I remember correctly.

I try to slip away quietly, but Eddie catches me at the door.

"Chef," he says. "I'm having a little get together at my place tonight. I'd like you to come."

"I don't know, Eddie," I say, trying to think of an excuse, any excuse, which is pointless because everyone knows that I have no life.

"It would mean a lot to me," he says. "and I wanted to talk to you about something."

Probably wants to buy me out of my show, the rat.

"Please," he says. "I swear you will not regret it."

Sigh. It is useless to fight this. And I know it.

"Okay. Sure, Eddie," I say. "I'll drop in for a little while."

"Great. Thanks." He grabs my hand in a firm shake. "Come by around eight."

He walks off to rejoin his adoring public. I head for my car.

Damn it.

A party at the hippie's place.

Well, it's a small price to pay, I suppose, in the war to regain control of my life. And if I eventually lose the war, that's fine. I've had a good run. I've heard retirement is not so bad.

What the hell am I thinking. That's

crazy talk.

I take out my iPod, put the tiny speakers in my ears. I browse through the track list and select a song. I hit play.

I can't tell you which song. I'm not even paying attention.

I'm just blocking out the fucking world.

A SORT OF SURPRISE PARTY

Okay. I've been standing in the hall, in front of the hippie's door for about ten minutes. Just staring at it. I can't seem to bring myself to knock.

I really don't want to be here. But it's important. I need to make every effort to show that I am cooperating with the current status quo.

I take a deep breath. I check for wrinkles in my shirt. I crack the knuckles on my left hand, and I knock on the fucking door.

There is no answer. I wait a moment, and knock again.

Nothing.

I look around. Is this the right place? I think so.

I place my ear against the door. Inside I hear loud rock music. People talking. I hear a laugh. I strain to listen harder when the door comes open, and I nearly stumble onto a very heavy-breasted young woman in a tank top. No bra. My god.

"I'm sorry," she says.

"No, no. It was all me," I say, embarrassed.

"You're Donovan Rushing."

"Yes," I say. "I am."

"My parents are huge fans of yours," she says, with a drunken grin. Her *parents*. Fantastic. Just peachy.

"That's great."

"Come inside, please," she says. "Eddie's been waiting for you."

I thank her and I step through the

door into the apartment. It's not as small as I remember. There are more pictures on the walls, strange paintings and artsy framed posters. A print of an antique absinthe poster catches my eye. For some reason he has a poster for the movie *Edward Scissorhands* on his wall. The creepy, pale face of Tom Cruise staring out at me.

There is a table with snacks. Mostly an assortment of chocolates and a rather impressive selection of cheese, as well as several types of crackers and fruits.

Another table has a wine selection. I take a glass and pour some from a bottle of European zinfandel. Ahh.. As long as the drink doesn't run out, this evening may be tolerable.

"Chef Rushing!"

I turn towards the voice, and the hippie is walking towards me.

"Hello Eddie," I say.

"I am so glad you could make it."

"I had nothing better to do," I say,

taking another drink, finishing off the glass.

"Well, please try and enjoy yourself," he says. "Later, when things quiet down I need to speak with you. It's important."

"Sure," I say. I pour another glass of wine. Shit. Second glass already. I need to reel it in a little if I want to survive this with any integrity intact.

I guess I should mingle. It's not really my crowd. Patrick, one of the production assistants from the show, is here. I gravitate towards him, and he welcomes me into his circle. Good. Safety in numbers. He introduces me to a gay lawyer, a couple of artists, a local architect, and an actor/musician named Jared Something-or-other from Louisiana. Apparently the CD player is currently blasting out songs from Jared's band's new album. I'm not impressed, but I don't show it. I smile and greet everyone. I sign a few autographs. Give cooking advice to a curious few people here and there.

I've done these parties before. I know how to play it out.

The wine helps.

A few hours later and I have put two bottles away by myself. The buzz is warm and nice. I am relaxed. I am confident. I am even sort of enjoying myself.

I really need to piss.

I find a hallway, always a good place to find a bathroom. The first door I try is apparently Eddie's bedroom. When I open the door I see two men engaging in oral sex. I think one of them is the lawyer I met. They pay me no mind. I close the door and try the next. It's locked. Dammit. There is light coming from under the door. This has to be it. Someone's inside. I wait a moment, then start to bang on the door.

"Could you please hurry in there," I plead. "I really need to go."

"That's Eddie's office," a female voice says from behind me.

I turn, and it's the girl who had let me in earlier. With the large tits. "The bathroom is the next one," she says. "I gotta pee too. You wanna share?"

I say nothing. She takes my hand and leads me into the bathroom. She pulls down her pants and sits down on the toilet. She smiles and sighs as her piss streams down into the water.

"My boyfriend left with some other bitch," she tells me.

"I'm sorry."

"Yeah.." She sits with her eyes closed. Then she smiles. "Come here."

She pulls me in front of her and begins to unbutton my pants.

"What are you doing?"

"What do you think?" She asks, as she gropes my throbbing penis and leans forward into it.

Oh. My. Fucking. God.

It has been a long time. A really long time. I am in my sixties. This girl is barely in her twenties. And she is sucking me off. I cum within two minutes. She swallows and laughs.

"What's so funny?" I ask.

"I was going to ask for your autograph," she says. "For my parents. But I was too nervous."

She laughs again. I laugh too. We are both laughing, loud and hard. Then she stops. She jumps up, drops to her knees and spews her stomach into the toilet.

Her perfect ass bent over, her shaved vagina smiling vertically up at me from between her legs. I wait for her vomiting to stop.

"Are you okay?" I ask.

"I'll be fine," she says. She stands up and pulls up her pants.

"Thanks," I say. "For the, uhm.."

"Blowjob? No problem," she says smiling. "You looked like you could use it."

"Yes. Well.."

"See you later, Chef," she says, slipping out of the bathroom.

Finally. I piss. Jesus Christ. That was wonderful.

I rejoin the party, feeling much better. I look around for the girl, but she has apparently disappeared. Oh well. Maybe she'll turn up later. I head for the wine table, skip the glass, and take a bottle. A freshly opened Chardonnay. A quarter of the bottle is gone in seconds. Yes. This party is all right.

A few more hours of mingling and drinking, and eating cheese and signing napkins and posing for cell phone camera photos, and midnight passes. Most of the people head out, in search of bigger parties or more intimate ones. The musician left with his CD, and the radio is tuned to an AM station. Over the airwaves some man is interviewing a woman who claims to have had contact with an alien or some shit.

In a daze, I go looking for the bathroom again. When I get to the door, it is locked. I knock, but don't hear a reply. I knock again. Dammit, someone must have passed out inside. I am too fucking wasted for this bullshit. I ram the door with my shoulder. I do it again. And again.

After a minute or so, my shoulder aching, the door gives way. I step inside and quickly realize that this is not the bathroom. It's a small office. Eddie's office. Dammit. There is a computer on a desk, and a small file cabinet. There are notebooks everywhere.

And then I notice something else.

Photographs. There are photographs all over the place. Photographs of me. Some new. Some old. Very old. Candid. Paparazzi-style spy photos. Photos of me and Abigail. Photos of Abigail alone. Photos of my friends, their friends, an elaborate family tree of associations.

What the hell is this?

"Donovan, I can explain this."

Eddie Blake. The hippie. Standing in the door behind me. When I turn to him, my eye is drawn to another set of photos on the wall.

Autopsy photos. Of Abigail. "Eddie," I say in calm shock. "Please move out of my way." My eyes do not leave the photos.

"This looks bad, I know," he says.

I punch him in the face. "Bad?! This looks bad?!"

He grabs his nose, gushing with blood.

"You sick degenerate piece of shit!" I hit him again, in the stomach. He doubles over. "What is this Eddie? Are you some twisted fucking stalker or something?"

"No!" he cried.

"Perverted fuck," I say, punching him in the face again. This time he falls to the floor in the hall, moaning.

I step out of the office and shut the door. I don't want anyone else seeing this shit. I grab another bottle of wine, Pinot Grigio this time, and I walk out of the apartment. I slam the door on my way out.

This is too much. I just don't care anymore. They can have the show. They can have it all. I am fucking done.

Somehow I make it to my car without falling down. I climb in, hit the gas, squealing out onto the street. I weave in and out of traffic, downing the wine. My cell phone rings. Eddie Blake. Out the fucking window.

I drive to the airport. I buy a ticket for New York. I pay cash. When I get there, I'll buy another ticket. For Paris. One way. Cash. In a few hours I'll be asleep on a very long flight.

Everyone I know can go fuck themselves. I'm sick of it all. I take a seat in the lobby. I take out my iPod, insert my earphones, and hit play.

Nothing. The batteries are dead.

Son of a fucking bitch.

VIN

THE DONOVAN RUSHING GUIDE
TO MUSIC CRITICISM

I may never run out of things to say in expression of my love for France. France is quite simply the most beautiful and inspiring country in all of Europe, with Spain being a close number two. To put it mildly, France is Wonderland. Eden. Oz.

And Paris especially, in my own humble opinion, would be a top contender for Capitol Of The World if not for my beloved New York. The markets, the cafes, the rich history. The brilliance of this city is unmatched. Unparalleled. While it's heyday as the Shangri La of culinary perfection may be long past, Paris still has much to offer for the hungry, well-informed, and well-paying traveler.

I have been in Paris for going on three weeks now. I have no phone. No real address. Just my passport and some cash I had stashed here over the years in a safety deposit box. I exchanged the cash for Euros, and while my financial cushion suffered a little due to the exchange rate, I still have more than enough to remain here for a few months. Alone. In complete isolation.

Well, not completely alone. I am friends with a number of chefs in the city, and they have agreed to help me keep a low profile for now. I am currently fast on my way to one of my favorite restaurants in the city, Peu Âgé Verge. I have an extreme yearning for their wild rabbit stew, and I am hoping to get the chef, Marcus Fuqualli, to join me for drinks during their afternoon break.

Not that I really need a drink. I awoke at six this morning, and I have been drinking ever since. It's another thing I love about this city. No one cares if you have a few too many glasses of wine, or shots of bourbon, or bottles of slick Japanese beer. You can walk around all day with a bottle of Chardonnay if you like, as long as you don't look like a homeless person.

Yes, my buzz is strong. And I am so calm. So relaxed. Not a care in the world. My worries back in the States are but a distant memory. An annoyance with no relevance to the here and now.

And then, out of the corner of my eye, I see it. The record store. With rock music posters in the window. One in particular stops me dead in my tracks. There is an image of a freakish skull with tusks, a horned helmet, and chains hanging from the sides. It is pretentiously heavy metal. Above the image, in stylized font, is a single word.

Motörhead.

What. The. Fucking. Fuck.

I go inside and approach the college dropout behind the counter.

"Do you speak English?"

"Oui," he says. "Yes."

"There is a poster in your window," I explain. "It says Motörhead."

"Yes."

"I have to ask," I say. "This has been irritating me. What the fuck is a Motörhead?"

"Eet eez a Breetish hevee metuhll band," he slurs.

"I have never heard of them. Are they famous?"

"Unconventionalee yes. Veree influential, for uhm, other metuhll bands."

This is no help at all. Why would someone continuously vandalize my car back in Los Angeles with odes to some British rock group. It's ridiculous to think about.

The young man just stares at me. Does he recognize me? I doubt it. I'm not Eddie Blake, hippie fucking extraordinaire. I stare back at him. He just stares back. This goes on for almost a minute.

I think he may be a homosexual. I hope I am not giving him the wrong idea. What with all the staring.

The Parisian nitwit finally shows me to the CD section, and points out the Motörhead albums. He picks up one titled "Ace Of Spades."

"Thees eez their most popyoularr album, but thees other one eez my personuhll favoreet."

He reaches for another CD. This one titled "Bomber."

"Would you like to leessuhn?"

"Sure. Why not," I say, regretting my reply instantly.

He takes the CD to the in-store stereo and pops the disc in. He hits play and the store is bombarded by bass heavy, loud, fast punkish heavy metal.

Yes, I know what punk music is. I lived in New York during the seventies, remember. I still have nightmares about the New York Dolls. If you know who that is, you'll understand.

This Motörhead music is god fucking

awful. The singer sounds like a monster from a Jim Henson puppet show. It's just terrible. Pathetic.

"I'll take all the Motörhead albums you have in stock," I say.

I leave the store with eleven CDs, five vinyl records, and even a couple cassette tapes, and step out onto the sidewalk. I then drop the purchases to the ground, and proceed to stomp them. The plastic cracks, the paper crumbles, more and more with each stomp. Soon, I am not merely stomping, but jumping up and down, laughing, smashing the heavy metal garbage into oblivion. A small crowd gathers, mostly young trashy rockers, gabbing on their cell phones in French. They remind me of that hippie, Eddie Blake.

Fuck Eddie Blake. And fuck these miscreants. I pick up a handful of shattered plastic and hurl it at the onlookers.

"Fuck Motörhead!" I exclaim before running off.

My god. That was amazing. I have never felt this good, this free. Like I can do anything I want. No one telling me what to do, what to say, where to be. No one calling the shots.

Except me. Donovan Rushing. Chef. Restaurateur. Crazy fucking lunatic extraordinaire.

And now, it's on to the restaurant, Peu Âgé Verge. I really worked up a little appetite. But I think I'll skip the food. It's time to celebrate. Drinks for everyone. Let the liquor flow.

Compliments of the fucking chef.

THE WORST DAY IN
DONOVAN RUSHING'S LIFE

One shot. Two shots. Three shots. Do me a favor and just leave the fucking bottle.

Thanks.

I am sitting at the bar in L'Église Du Plaisir, a jazz club near the Seine. Groovy place, supposedly. I wouldn't know, as I have not looked up from the bar once since sitting down two hours ago.

I have been in a dreamy haze for an hour now. Thinking about Abigail Preponi. The love of my life. Would you like to know about the day she died?

Okay.

It was May 17, 1975. I was thirty-two years old. Abigail was barely twenty-three. I was hosting *The Cooking Hour with Donovan Rushing,* and we had recently become a nationally broadcast program. Ratings were pretty fair. I was starting to make a little extra money. It was nice.

I woke up early on this morning to head down to the fish market, put some orders in, pick up a few items for our own kitchen. Gordon Hessler, who had been my manager for about four years then, called me before I was ready to leave. He said he needed me to come to his office for a meeting with one of the TV producers. I tried to talk my way out of it, but it was no use.

I woke Abigail and asked her to go to the market for me. I gave her a shopping list. I poured her some coffee. And I kissed her goodbye.

At the meeting, we went over recipes for upcoming episodes, we discussed possible advertising ideas, and as always Gordon brought up his desire for the show to change its name to *The Main Course.* I really didn't care. The meeting seemed like so many others. Pointless and tedious.

It wasn't until I arrived back at the apartment that I felt something was wrong. A half hour later, Gordon called me. He had heard from a contact at the police department.

Abigail was dead.

She had made it to the market. Bought the items I requested. On her way back she was gunned down from a moving car. It was early. Very little traffic. No witnesses. The killer got away with no problem.

I can remember dropping the phone and running towards the door. And that's all. I was found a little while later, laying unconscious at the bottom of the stairwell in my apartment building. I had tripped and knocked myself out, or had passed out and fell. I never found out for sure.

I went to the hospital. I identified my wife's body. She had four bullet holes in her chest. She looked peaceful. And so pale. I thought to myself, *She needs to eat some red meat.*

Then I vomited on the doctor standing beside me.

Then I had a drink. Or maybe twelve. I didn't bother counting.

I took a week off from work. I was the head chef at La Tabouret Courant. I had met Abigail there in 1970. We had been married for four years. In one hour, my life was over.

Her funeral was small and private. Her murder was anything but. National newspaper and TV reporters descended upon my neighborhood. They were everywhere. I was a household name overnight.

My ratings skyrocketed.

I couldn't take it. I returned to work early. I was offered a few months off. I declined. I had to cook. And keep cooking. Never stop.

Abigail's killer was out there. It had to be personal. Somehow connected to my vague association with a few mobsters. Not that I was a gangster. I was a local celebrity chef. You meet people. Some of these people are not so squeaky clean. Of course I used my connections to try and find any leads in the investigation of my wife's murder, but nothing was ever found. Whoever was responsible for Abigail's death was long gone. Luckily, Gordon was there to help me through it. Kept my mind on my work. On my career, which only flourished.

Abigail's death was a blessing to my career, and a curse on my mind and soul. Most of the money I made in that first year was spent on alcohol. Lots of alcohol. All kinds. From around the world.

I was drinking to keep her out of my mind. Then I drank too much, and I couldn't think of anything else but her. And her smile. Her laugh. Her cold, peaceful, pale body.

Then, I'd drink more to forget again.

And now. I am in Paris. An alcoholic's dreamland. I just might drink myself into oblivion here.

And I don't care. Perhaps I will get to see her again soon. My Abigail.

I hope it's soon. I'm so lonely. And tired.

And thirsty.

"Bartender," I say. "Can I get another bottle, *por vavor*?"

THE BOWELS OF PARIS

Okay. The honeymoon is officially over. Thirty-one days in Paris and I am broke. I paid for two more weeks at the hotel, and I had seventy Euros left. Enough to buy some food for the next week, or one bottle of acceptable wine.

I bought the wine, of course. That was last night. And this is today.

I awoke on the bathroom floor around ten this morning, and I have spent the last couple of hours walking around various neighborhoods in the city. When I get hungry enough, I'll be able to get a free meal from a familiar restaurant, but getting more than a few comped glasses of wine may prove to be a little trickier.

Free beers after dark will be no problem, but that will only satisfy me for so long. I have been spoiled with the good stuff. Like a heroin addict settling for some cheap marijuana mixed with oregano leaves.

A lot of oregano. You get the idea.

I have never been a sober person. But I kept myself in check for years. Social drinking, a glass to unwind after a long day. But after moving to Los Angeles, I have to admit that, slowly, I started depending on it more and more.

Much like after Abigail died. I spent three years in a drunkard's haze. At the urging of Gordon and my dear friend Carlos I went into counseling. It took nearly a year, but I overcame the addiction.

But it was always there. Every once in a while I would let my guard down, have too many drinks, make a fool of myself. Especially on my secret vacations, where I was treated like royalty for a week. Anything I wanted, it was always available. As long as I was available to my host. Which was always.

Where the hell am I anyway?

This is further east than I normally go. Pretty shitty neighborhood. Reminds me of Harlem when I was a kid. Or most of Philadelphia now. Smells like shit.

I see a group of Muslim women on the opposite sidewalk. I pray that they are not strapped with bombs. And then I immediately hate myself for thinking that. Not all Muslims are terrorists.

Then again.. Note to self: *avoid the pizza shops*.

A couple of black men on the corner ahead. Look like drug dealers. Good thing I'm broke. Can't get robbed.

But it's the middle of the day. I shouldn't have to worry. I'm just hung-over. And lost. No big deal. Keep walking, and you will end up somewhere.

I turn around. Felt like someone was following me. I don't see anyone suspicious. At least no more suspicious than everyone else walking around.

Strange strangers eyeing me strangely. I haven't showered in a week. I haven't changed clothes in three days. I smell like shit. I look like shit. I'm hungry.

And I'm thirsty. So fucking thirsty.

Oh god, I need a drink. I am about to go out of my fucking mind. What little of it I have left.

God dammit. What's a man have to do? Sell his soul for a drink?

"Donovan." A voice behind me. I fucking knew it.

I turn around. No one. Nothing. No, not nothing. Something.

On a bench, not twenty feet behind me, I see it. A half pint bottle of scotch.

The bottle said my name. It's been following me.

I approach it cautiously. I pick it up. There is a note underneath. It is folded. On the outside it reads "Drink up."

And I do. Oh god. Yes.. It burns going down. It is perfect. I am almost crying.

I open the note. There is an address. And a makeshift map. And a simple message. "Follow me for more. I have what you need."

Sounds good to me. I start walking.

The directions lead me to a desolate building a few blocks away. Very uninviting, but someone went to the trouble of getting me here, so I suppose I should go inside.

"Hello?" It's dark inside. My voice echoes. Can this be the right place?

I see a light come on in a room down the hall to my right. I head towards it. I reach the door and look inside. There is an electric lamp on the floor of the otherwise empty room.

"I am Donovan Rushing," I say. "You left me a note."

No answer.

I'm getting a little spooked now. I back out of the room to leave. I turn and there is a man standing in the darkness of the hall. I can't really see him, but he's holding something.

"Did you leave the note?" I ask.

He extends his hand, which I now see is holding a bottle of wine. Château d'Yquem. 1893. A ten thousand dollar bottle of wine.

Sweet Jesus Fucking Christ.

He just stands there. No movement.

"Well," I say, moving slowly towards him. Towards his hand. Towards the wine. "Thank you very much."

I reach for the bottle. I miss. No. I don't miss. He pulls it away. He raises it up and swings.

Fast. And hard.

I barely realize what is happening when the bottle shatters upon the top of my head, and the sweet and bitter musky wine

203

pours down my face, into my eyes. It's smell clouds the atmosphere.

As I fall to the floor my only thought is of the wine.

"What a fucking waste," I whisper before blacking out.

THINGS I NEVER EXPECTED
TO HEAR

At first I think it must be the throbbing, nearly unbearable in my head, that wakes me up. But it's not. It's the smell. Someone is cooking. And it smells delicious.

I groan and try to reach for my head, to caress the throbbing area, but I can't. My arms are tied down to the chair I now realize I am sitting in.

"I'll untie you in a few minutes," a voice from my left says. "When I am sure you will be cooperative."

I look to the left, and I see a kitchen. Standing at the stove, in a white t-shirt and blue jeans, is Eddie Blake.

The fucking hippie. My stalker. And now, it would seem, my kidnapper.

"Where am I?"

"We are in the apartment of a friend of mine," he says, never looking up from the large black pot he is tending to. "She is out of town, and I had a spare key."

"Why are you doing this?"

"Because we need to talk, Chef."

"How did you find me?"

He stops and looks at me. On his shirt is a womanly-looking man with a microphone, and the words IGGY POP. Whatever the hell that means. "A few days ago someone uploaded a video clip from their cell phone to the internet. It showed you going ape shit on a pile of Motörhead CDs."

"God dammit."

"Yeah," he says. "I've been to Paris more than a few times. I recognized the neighborhood in the background."

"Why did you smash my head with a fucking wine bottle?"

"Would you have come willingly?"

"No."

He nods at me and continues cooking. I look around the apartment. It is small. Typical for Paris. To my right is the living room. On the TV is a James Stewart movie. *Vertigo*. Late 50s Hitchcock thriller. The sound is muted, and there are French subtitles on the screen. *Une seule est un vagabond. Deux ensemble sont toujours quelque part.*

"Eddie," I say. "Are you going to kill me?"

The hippie releases a squealing laugh from the kitchen. "Why the hell would I want to kill you?"

"I don't know," I say. "Some sort of *Fatal Attraction* thing."

"Okay," he says, coming out of the kitchen. "Let me explain this to you."

He kneels down on the floor in front of me. "I'm not crazy. And I'm not kidnapping you. This is more like an intervention."

"This is really fucked up is what it is."

"I know that," he says. "But I needed to be sure that all of my information was correct before bringing it to you."

"What information?"

"Hold on," he says. "I'm getting to that."

He sits silently for a few minutes, apparently gathering his thoughts. My god, he really looks like a fucking psychopath.

"When I was a kid," he begins, "I wanted to be Batman. Not because he had a cool cape and a cool car, but because he was The World's Greatest Detective. I mean, his comic book was even called *Detective Comics*."

"What the fuck are you…"

"No!" he shouts. "You have to listen. You see, I wanted to be a detective. I wanted to solve mysteries and gather clues and right wrongs. But it never happened. Dreams of grandeur as a musician, as an actor, as a rebel took over. Until 1985, while I was working at your restaurant. Something I overheard caught my attention. Something dark. Something suspicious."

"I don't know what the hell it is you are talking about."

"Do you remember Virginia McVay?"

Virginia. There's a name I haven't heard in a while. We dated briefly. The only real relationship I ever had after Abigail's death a decade earlier. Sweet girl.

"Yes," I say. "Of course I remember her. What does she have to do with anything?"

"She was at the restaurant the night I quit," he says. "In your office with another man. I didn't catch the full conversation, but he said to her 'you have your whole life ahead of you. You don't want to end up like the last one.'"

Okay. The hippie has my attention.

"The man handed her an envelope and she ran out crying. I believe she broke up with you the next day."

"Yes," I say. "I think you're right. But what you are telling me doesn't make any sense."

"Virginia was paid to leave you," Eddie says.

"That's ridiculous," I say. "And even if it were true, why would I care now?"

"Because the man who paid her off was our manager, Gordon Hessler."

"So," I say. "You solved the mystery. Do you want a prize?"

"That wasn't the mystery."

"Enlighten me, Eddie. What's the fucking mystery?"

"The mystery is Abigail, Chef."

"Abigail…"

"*The last one.* The night I quit, I went to work. All the years I put in, in the various restaurants and bars, on television production sets with producers and assistants and reporters, I was gathering the information. Putting together the pieces. And I did it."

"You did what?"

"I figured it out," he says. "I found the man who killed your wife."

I am speechless. My throat is dry. Has this man lost his mind? He can see me struggling to say something, and he stands up, goes to a table and opens a folder. He brings over to me a photograph of a man. A police photo.

"This is Alvin Burnell," the hippie says. "He was executed six months ago at a prison in Texas. He was locked up for killing the wife of a lawyer in Austin. He had been paid by the lawyer, paid to kill, so that the lawyer and his new girlfriend could run off together. Alvin Burnell was suspected in the death of a woman in Florida in the early 1980s. This woman's husband collected millions in life insurance. And this man, this killer, Alvin Burnell, just happened to be living in New York City in 1975. Just two blocks from the spot where Abigail Rushing was gunned down in the early morning hours."

Tears fill my eyes. "How do you know?"

"How do I know he did it?" he says. "Because he told me. I visited him in prison a month before his execution. I told him the information would not go public, would not lead to more charges against him. There were financial incentives as well. I told him I would send money to his family. His sister and nieces and nephews."

"You made a deal with the man who killed my wife?"

"I needed his help. I needed his testimony to my case. I needed the name. The name of the man who paid him to kill your wife. I had my suspicion, but I needed him to say it."

"I don't think I want to hear anymore," I say.

"He wrote it down, right here."

Eddie holds up a sheet of paper. In bad handwriting are the words that will forever haunt me. The words that instantly make me sick in the deepest pits of my soul.

Gordon Hessler is the man who paid me to kill Abigail Rushing. He offered me $20,000 in May of 1975. I accepted his offer. I killed the woman. Mr. Hessler never paid me. Fuck him.

Signed *Alvin Burnell.*

I try to talk. Try to argue, but the only thing that comes out is vomit. Weeks of wine and brandy and other liquors. I just keep spewing, for nearly five minutes, until I am just dry heaving. Nothing left inside. Nothing left at all.

"I am sorry," Eddie finally says. And he means it. I can tell.

He unties my hands, and fetches me a damp towel. I clean myself off.

"I have two tickets to Los Angeles," he says. "I want you to go with me. We can face Gordon together."

"No," I say. "I can't."

"Yes, you can, Chef. You have to."

"No," I say again. "First we must go to New York. I know people who owe me favors."

I stand up. A little dizzy, but thinking clearly for the first time in weeks. For the first time in years.

"If we are going to do this, we have to do it right."

"Whatever you want," Eddie says.

Yes. Whatever I want. First, New York to cash in my chips. Then, Los Angeles.

The fucking German has some explaining to do.

LA VIANDE ET DU SANG COURS

THE DONOVAN RUSHING AND EDDIE BLAKE SCHOOL OF KIDNAPPING

Two days in New York. That is all it took. One hour with one very influential individual, and the preparations came together.

Now, I am in Los Angeles. With Eddie Blake. Still a hippie. But also a friend now. Two men have come with us from New York. One is named Vinnie. The other goes by the moniker Brute.

I know what you're thinking. Donovan Rushing, the great TV chef, made some terrible deal with a mafia boss. That I sold my sold my soul to the mob.

You are wrong. I made no deal. Like I

said, I went to New York to cash in my chips.

It is October 25. Escoffier's birthday. 6:00 AM. I am sitting in a rental car across the street from Gordon Hessler's house. My manager. My producer. My friend for over thirty years.

And now, the target of my vile hatred. The muse of my vitriol. This slimy German cunt is responsible of the murder of my wife Abigail in 1975. And I am going to find out why.

At two minutes after, like clockwork, Gordon steps out through his front door in his running suit. It is four miles to the park. This is his routine. Every other day. The jog.

I watch Gordon take to the sidewalk. I allow him a block or so before I start to follow. I pick up my cell phone and hit speed dial number one.

"Eddie," I say into the phone. "The German is on the move. Are the Sicilians ready?"

"Yes, Chef," Eddie replies. "We will

be waiting for your first move."

I hang up the phone and speed up. I am tempted to just run off the road, mow the bastard down and get it over with, but I keep going, passing him up. I arrive at Continental Park with a half hour to spare.

I get a cup of coffee. I feel like I should get some alcohol, but to be honest, I don't really want it. I haven't desired a drink since leaving Paris. The coffee is good. Rich. Dark. Bitter. Cheap.

I check my watch. I should get into position.

I go to the walking bridge in the center of the park. Another sidewalk runs under it. This is part of Gordon's jogging route. I check my watch again and look up. And there he is. God dammit, Gordon. Why have you put me in this situation?

I look around for the others. I see no one. It's kind of funny, these big, dumb gangster heavies hiding like fucking ninjas.

Gordon approaches the bridge. I reach into my pocket. Just as he makes it under the bridge's shadows, I step out.

"Gordon."

He stops abruptly. "Donovan?" He looks very surprised. Confused. "What are you doing here? Where the hell have you been?"

"We need to talk," I say.

"About what?"

"About Abigail."

He just looks at me. "What are you talking about, Donovan? What's wrong?"

I pull the gun with the silencer from my pocket. Just something else I picked up in New York. I had a lot of chips to cash.

"What the hell is going on here?" he says. "Are you drunk?"

"No," I say. "I am as sober as a baby wolf."

I aim, and I fire. A muffled shot pops out and the bullet shatters Gordon's left knee cap. Blood sprays in all directions. And he screams. Or at least he tries to.

Like ghosts, Vinnie and Brute are on him. Brute grabs Gordon from behind, and Vinnie shoves a ball gag into his mouth. I look up at Eddie, standing on the bridge. He drops a cloth sack down to me. It is soaked with chloroform. I run up and throw the sack over Gordon's head. He fights for a few seconds, but he has no choice. His body gives in, goes limp.

Brute picks Gordon up, while Vinnie gets the van. An inconspicuous white cargo van. Gordon is tossed into the back and we are on the road before even the grass in the park knew we were there.

You know, one of the less than admirable things about Los Angeles are all the disgusting, abandoned buildings where crackheads and cock-sucking squatters and Mexican gang members spend their nights hiding from cops. But still, these derelict places have their certain charm. Nobody worth paying attention to hangs out here. The human trash is easily scared off by guns and the two bodyguard-like gangsters in my entourage.

And so it is in the basement of some undisclosed location where we have brought Gordon Hessler. We have hurled him into a dank room, with a battery-powered lantern in the corner, and the moment he wakes up I send in the Sicilians. With a pair of baseball bats, they proceed to rain their hits and whacks down upon the helpless German. With his left leg incapacitated, he wobbles around on the dirty floor, moaning loudly from behind the ball gag.

He looks like a giant tuna, flopping around on the deck of a fishing boat, while large Sicilian fishermen beat it half to death.

I am starting to feel a little hungry.

Blood fills his eyes. Sweat soaks his shirt. Piss stains his running pants. He cries for mercy, but there is none.

Donovan Rushing shows no mercy. But after five minutes of beating, I walk in to stop it. Vinnie and Brute back off as I kneel down to Gordon. I remove the ball gag.

"Fuck!" he screams.

"Why did you do it, Gordon?"

"What?" he is hyperventilating. "What did I do?"

"You had Abigail killed, you piece of shit. Why?"

"That's ridiculous, Donovan. I…"

I slap him across the face. I reach into my pocket for the photo of Alvin Burnell.

"This is the man who killed my wife."

Gordon looks at the photo. I can see, in his eyes, his fear growing.

"I have never seen that man," he cries.

I take out the note.

"This was written by him. He said you paid him to do it."

"I would have never hurt her, Donovan," Gordon says. "I loved her like family."

I take out the gun and aim it at his head.

"No, Donovan!"

"Just tell me you are sorry, Gordon."

"I didn't do it," he cries.

"JUST TELL ME YOU ARE FUCKING SORRY YOU FUCKING SON OF A BITCH!"

"I'm sorry!" Gordon finally screams.

We both go silent. We stare at each other.

"I'm sorry," he whimpers.

Disgusting son of a bitch.

"No. Not yet you aren't."

"Donovan," he says. "Are you sure you want to do this?"

I calmly collect myself. This is it. This is where I take my stand.

"I have never been more sure of anything, Gordon. This is the way it has to be."

I swing and knock Gordon over the head with the gun. He drops to the floor.

Out fucking cold.

"Eddie," I say.

"Yes, Chef?"

"I'm going to need a kitchen."

THE LAST SUPPER

Five hours, seventeen hundred dollars, one gas powered grill and one lovely set of knives later, I am beginning to cook.

It is essentially a pork loin recipe. One I've prepared more times than I can remember. Eddie and Vinnie managed to find all the spices and herbs I requested.

This is going to be Gordon Hessler's last meal. Even now, I do not want to disappoint. I am a chef. Professional and practical.

The meat will need to cook for about three and a half hours. Seasoned with kosher salt, fresh ground black pepper, basil, minced garlic and olive oil, wrapped in foil, sitting in the portable grill at about

226

three hundred degrees.

In the meantime, Eddie and I work on the side dishes. Collard greens, a favorite of Gordon's, cooked in a portable steamer, brown rice with shiitake mushrooms, making use of the portable rice cooker and a second steamer, and some French bread drizzled with olive oil wrapped in foil to be placed on the grill near the end of the loin's cooking time.

And to drink, a delightful Pinot Grigio from Spain. Eddie picked up a bottle of Jägermeister for himself, of which I did not approve and moderately scolded him. I'll be having a Sprite, should I decide that I am thirsty.

Time flies quickly when cooking, to me at least. The meat is just about done. The bread goes into the grill.

I give an injection into Gordon's arm, some more shit from New York, and Gordon begins to stir from his knock-out-induced slumber. He is sitting in a wheelchair at a small dining table. He looks around in a daze. He doesn't appear to be in any real pain.

Good. We'll save that for later.

"Hello, Gordon," I say calmly.

"Hey," Gordon replies. "What's that smell?"

He looks toward the grill on the other side of the room, near a ventilation shaft.

"I'm just making you something special," I say. It's taking every ounce of my will power to keep from just killing him right now. I could strangle him, with little force, or snap his neck.

"Gordon," I say. "I want to make it very clear that I am very disappointed in you. You are in a lot of trouble, old friend."

"Donovan..."

"No," I say. "Just listen. I have given you an injection. A sedative to relax you. Keep you in a sort of dreamlike haze. But it is also a pretty potent form of truth serum. You will not be able to lie to me anymore, Gordon. Now, how does that make you feel?"

"I feel… hungry."

"In a few minutes," I assure him. "First, let's talk."

I take a seat opposite the table from him. He looks so pathetic. An old, sad German. He looks homeless. Especially in that stained running suit. I really don't know how I ever trusted him, especially for so long.

"For over thirty years," I begin. "I have looked to you as a friend. As a brother. A father. A savior. You have always been there to hold me up when the world was trying to drag me down. But now I know it was all an act. You were the one dragging me down, Gordon. I let you pull the strings. I gave you total control of my entire life. And what did you do? You killed my wife. My Abigail."

I stare at him. He is beginning to shake. "Tell me why, Gordon?"

"You were destined for great things," he says. "I knew it from the start. From the moment I met you. But that woman. She was holding you back. She hated the TV show, she hated me. She never trusted me. With her gone, I knew you'd do what I said. And her death, the tragedy, it did what I knew it would do. It put a national spotlight on you. You were an overnight sensation. Her death was our shortcut to the top."

"Wow," Eddie says from behind me. "That was pretty fucking forthcoming."

I am so close to killing this man. *Abigail was our shortcut*?! What kind of fucked up logic is this fuck living with? I get up from the table and go to the grill. I take the meat and bread, set them to the side. I make a plate for Gordon. Two thick slices of the loin, and conservative portions of the sides. I pour the wine and then I serve my guest.

The dish is beautiful. Picture perfect. I am tempted to take a photo with my cell phone and send it to Ruth Reichl at Gourmet magazine. She would appreciate it.

"I put a lot of work into this," I say to Gordon. "I hope you enjoy it."

Slowly, Gordon takes his fork. The

meat is so tender a knife is unnecessary. And giving him a knife would be foolish of me anyway. He takes a bite, and even in his dire situation I can see that he still appreciates my culinary talents.

"Would you like to know what it is I do on my secret vacations?"

Gordon stops chewing, and looks at me in near disbelief. "Sure," he says.

I am sure that you would like to know as well. So let me share with you how it all started.

You will recall that Frank Sinatra became a great admirer of my cooking early in my career. He spoke highly of my meals to his friends, much of which were rather shady men with shady connections. One of those men was Antoine Kavelli, head of the Kavelli crime family long-based out of Brooklyn. A real Godfather. A despicable man, of course. But to be in his presence, to speak with him, was something special. Most people sought him out for work or favors or money. But it is something entirely different when Antoine Kavelli comes looking for you. It means trouble, usually.

And so it was in May of 1968 that Mr. Kavelli showed up at my apartment door. I was worried, naturally. Had I served him a bad oyster or an overcooked steak? I was not sure. All I knew was that I was nearly soiling myself as I opened the door to let him in.

Mr. Kavelli took a seat and I offered him a drink. He asked for a beer. Then he offered me a proposal. He was going to have a very important gathering in July. A week long family reunion at his estate on a private island in Reed's Bay off the Jersey coast. Near Atlantic City, where the Kavelli family is an important presence.

Mr. Kavelli asked me to be one of the organizers for the gathering. He said that I would be in charge of the menus for all of the meals. That I would be at his command for anything he needed, as far as food was concerned. In return, I would be treated as a guest, with all the perks and freedoms. Anything I needed, would be paid for. Anything I wanted, would be happily provided. And as payment, he would grant me one wish. Any favor I needed, would be honored with no questions asked.

As weary as I was about accepting a deal from a known mob boss, turning him down seemed an even worse idea. So I accepted. I had a week vacation coming up, so it would not interfere with my job, although I am sure Mr. Kavelli could have worked that out as well.

I spent that week on Mr. Kavelli's island overseeing so many cooks and other staff, it was almost maddening. There were hundreds and hundreds of guests, and I only saw Mr. Kavelli a handful of times my entire stay. But he was not lying. Anything I wanted, I received.

Alcohol. Women. Exotic spices. A thousand dollar pair of shoes from a distant Kavelli cousin I'd never even met before. No one disrespected me at all. It was fantastic. Otherworldly.

There were deals being made, crimes being planned, important people getting paid. I saw politicians, judges, lawyers, all manner of people. Even Sinatra stayed a few nights. It was the most powerful island on Earth for one week.

And then, on the next to last day, shots rang out. Someone had attempted to kill Mr. Kavelli, a traitor working for a rival family. The would-be assassin was gunned down and his body taken away. No one called the police. No one alerted the media. A few hours later, it was as if nothing had ever happened.

That night, Mr. Kavelli called me into his private quarters. When I arrived, Mr. Kavelli was standing near a table. On the table was the body of the gunman.

"This man," Mr. Kavelli said. "He was working for the Marichi family. They will not admit it, but I know it is true."

I really didn't know what to say. Why was he telling me this?

"I have invited them for dinner tomorrow," he continued. "We are going to discuss some things. Try to work out an arrangement."

Mr. Kavelli then turned to face me. He put his hands on my shoulders.

"You are the most talented, most

passionate chef I have ever met, Donovan. I am sorry if this disturbs you, but I have to ask. Can you do something with this?"

He motioned towards the body.

"You want me to get rid of it?" I asked.

"In a manner of speaking," he said. "Can you prepare it?"

Prepare it? And then it hit me. Oh god, did it ever.

"You want me to cook him?"

"Yes," Mr. Kavelli whispered. "I want to serve him to the Marichis."

I can remember the smell, the stench, of my own sweat soaking though my clothes.

"I am sorry to put you in this awkward situation," he said. "But this is important. And my family would be forever in your debt."

Out of fear, the same fear that made

me agree to come to the island in the first place, I said yes. I would cook the man.

Mr. Kavelli asked what I needed, and since I had never cooked a human before I sort of winged it. I said to have the body cleaned, skinned, and the meat removed from the torso and limbs. I requested the heart and the liver be removed as well.

This was the meat and organs that I felt I could work with. Pretend I was working with beef or pork. I left for my room, and began reviewing my cookbooks, trying not to let the thought of what I'd agreed to do drive me insane. I did not watch the butchering process, but the next day when I arrived at the kitchen and found the meat, I was surprised at how natural it seemed. It was just meat.

All I had to do was cook it. And I did. And it was served to the Marichi family.

Most of the meat was made into a stew, with seasonal vegetables and a pork-based broth. The liver was pan-seared in olive oil and served with ratatouille to Daniel Marichi, the eldest son of the family's patriarch Sergio Marichi, who was served the main dish of the roasted heart with steamed asparagus seasoned with minced onions. They said the food was delicious.

When they were told what they were eating, they were horrified. Then they had a private meeting with Mr. Kavelli.

They never crossed him again.

When it was all over, Mr. Kavelli handed me an envelope. There was five thousand in cash inside.

"If this is not enough," he said "you let me know."

Then I returned home. I went back to work at the restaurant. And I started drinking.

The next year, I was invited out to the island again. And once again, I found myself cooking some unlucky person. This time, it was a judge who had ruled against Mr. Kavelli's nephew, despite having been paid off.

The year after that, I cooked three

high ranking members of the rival Ginovini family from Las Vegas. The next year I met Abigail, and I skipped the Kavelli island getaway.

Abigail and I were married in 1971, and Mr. Kavelli paid for everything. No one knew, of course. Not even Abigail. It wasn't until 1975, after Abigail was killed, that I started to accept Mr. Kavelli's invitations again.

I quit asking where the meat came from. I just cooked it. Year after year. Every year since then.

I kept it a total secret. Not even Carlos, my best friend in the world, knew about my trips. Nobody knew.

Until I told Eddie Blake, on the flight from Paris. And he said that he understood. And that he would help me.

And then I called upon Vincent Kavelli, Antoine's son and now head of the family since his father's death in 1991. The family owed me favors. Lots of them. And I needed a big one. Vincent was more than happy to honor my needs.

"So tell me, Gordon," I say to the German seated before me. "How is your meal?"

He stops eating, and looks down at his plate. The food is nearly gone.

"You fed me human meat?"

"I did."

"Who was it?"

I motion for Eddie to come over. Eddie grabs Gordon's wheelchair by the handles and pulls him away from the table. Gordon's eyes instantly draw down towards his legs, what's left of them, and he starts to gag and choke.

His bare legs, exposed to the light, show considerable mutilation. His left thigh has been totally carved away, and rectangular strips from his right thigh and calf have been delicately removed.

Brute goes over to the CD player in the corner of the room and hits play. Loud heavy metal music blares out from the speakers. Motörhead. "Dead Men Tell No Tales."

"What the fuck have you done to my legs?!" Gordon screams.

"Your legs," I say. "Your fucking legs?!"

I grab a knife from a side table and I leap upon the filthy cunt.

"What have you done to my fucking life?!" I yell, as I plunge the knife into his shoulder. Gordon screams, tries to fight me, but the sedative I gave him is too strong.

"You killed my wife, Gordon!" I stab his hands which have risen up in defense.

"You took away the love of my fucking life!" I stab at his face, slicing his left cheek and ear.

"You disgusting, double-crossing, lying, treacherous, piece of fucking shit!" I stab and I stab.

With every cut, I feel a little more free. With every pint of blood, Abigail's rest grows more peaceful. With each slice of meat I pull away from bone, my appetite grows more satisfied.

Every finger wrenched from hand. Every eye gouged out. Every nerve stimulated with precise masterful agony. Every beat of his dying heart. I smile. I laugh. You would think that I had finally lost my mind.

But you would be wrong. I'm not crazy. I know exactly what I'm doing. My entire life has been a never ending parade of appetizers. Never enough to fill you up. Just enough to make you hungry for more.

But now, finally. After all these years. I have it. The main course. And it is delicious. The perfect meal. I am stuffed. I couldn't eat another bite.

I think I'll have seconds.

Gordon's throat opens wide and the sweet crimson flows. I thrust the knife into his chest, piercing his rotten fucking heart.

"Please," Gordon somehow manages to say. "Stop."

"I'll finish this," I say as his final breath bubbles out. "When I see you in Hell."

A bloody gasp escapes his lungs as I twist the knife. Blood pours for several minutes, until the German is as white as a handful of sea salt.

And now, it is done. It is over.

I just sit, staring at the mess I have made. I feel like I should be throwing up, but I'm fine. I breathe calmly. Brute turns off the CD player. The song wasn't even over yet. That's how quickly I have worked.

I get up. Eddie hands me a damp towel. I wipe my face and hands. I tell Brute and Vinnie to get to work. They take knives from a leather case and begin to work on Gordon. I didn't mention that Brute and Vinnie are also line cooks at one of my New York restaurants, did I?

I make my way up the stairs, step outside and lean against a wall. I close my eyes. And I think of Abigail.

She would not have liked what I've just done. Not at all. But that's okay. I can let her go now.

I start to cry. Harder than I ever have before. Even at Abigail's funeral, I did not cry like this.

"Chef," Eddie says. He is standing in the doorway. "Are you alright?"

"No, Eddie. I am certainly not alright. But I'm getting close."

"We'll be done in about ten minutes," he says.

I nod to him, and he returns to the basement. He's a good guy, that Eddie Blake. I was hard on him before. Too hard. He was just a hippie. Now, he's my accomplice. My secret-sharer. And a friend for life.

I reach into my pocket for my iPod. I put on the headphones and hit play.

Hank Williams. "Hey Good Lookin'."

I smile, and I think of Abigail again.

This was her favorite song. She used to sing it to me all the time.

"Goodbye, good lookin'," I say.

And then, I head back down to the basement, to help gather my things, and close the book on the worst chapters of my life. Because next, is a whole new chapter. A whole new book.

A book to be filled with recipes for a happy life.

DONOVAN RUSHING APOLOGIZES
TO NO ONE

"This crowd is fucking insane," Eddie says.

"They are probably here to see me," I joke.

Eddie Blake and I are looking out the window of his new Manhattan restaurant, Hellfire Grub. It is a joint venture. I am putting up the money, he's putting up the menu. There are hundreds of people gathered outside, waiting for the doors to open in one hour. Waiting for Eddie's new menu of spicy and sinful dishes.

It's been four months since our bloody task in the slums of Los Angeles. Four months since I held a meeting and cancelled *The Main Course* from television

245

broadcast. Two months since the search for Gordon Hessler was called off. Two months since buying this building for Eddie and helping him design the restaurant.

It is Valentine's Day. Mine and Abigail's wedding anniversary. Later today I will drive out to the cemetery. Pay my respects. Leave a box of dark chocolate truffles. And then go home.

I'm not even sticking around for Eddie's opening night. This is his baby. I am confident in his capabilities.

In all my life, I struggled between what I wanted and what others wanted for me. And what others wanted *from* me. Now, I am just Donovan Rushing. Just a guy who owns a lot of restaurants. A guy who likes jazz. A guy who has been sober for four months.

And I am happy. I have no real responsibility. I can just… be.

My cell phone rings. Excuse me.

"Hello?"

"Donovan," my friend Carlos says on the other end. "Are you still leaving Eddie alone tonight?"

"Yes," I say. "There is no need for me to stick around."

"Great. Listen, you remember Heather Christian? The singer?"

"Yeah… with the piano?"

"That's her," he says. "She's got a show tonight. Some little artsy performance hall. I'm gonna check it out. You want to tag along?"

"I don't know," I say. "I gotta go to Abigail's grave, and I was going to take it easy."

"Since when does Donovan Rushing take anything easy?"

I laugh. He's right.

"Okay," I say. "But you have to promise not to hit on her."

"Scout's honor," he says. I'm sure his

fingers are crossed behind his back.

I hang up the phone, and try to resume my conversation. But there is no one around. I *was* talking to someone wasn't I?

Or was I talking to myself?

I think I was. "I am terribly sorry," I say.

I laugh to myself. That was ridiculous.

Donovan Rushing apologizes to no one.

LES ENTREMETS

This final section of the book is a collection of extras that are meant to add to the overall enjoyment of the book. Much like DVDs usually showcase their *special bonus features*, I feel that more authors and publishers should take the initiative to give a little more bang for their readers' buck. It is in everyone's best interest to give people more reasons to read, other than just the story itself.

THE ODD COUPLE

An afternoon with Eddie Blake and
Donovan Rushing

Article by Conrad Mizelli. Originally
printed in *Coolinary Times* magazine issue
#138.

WHEN I WAS OFFERED THE CHANCE
to spend a few hours interviewing
celebrity chef icon Eddie Blake at his cult
hit Manhattan restaurant Hellfire Grub, I
knew it was a once in a lifetime
opportunity. The fan favorite chef rarely
gives interviews, and he's only given one
in the year since his restaurant opened.
But, as Bob Dylan sang, things have
changed.

I am waiting in the lobby of the

eccentric bar and grill, checking my watch, noting that Chef Blake is twenty minutes late. I am beginning to wonder if he's decided not to show. And then a familiar voice catches me off guard.

"Eddie says he's sorry that he's running late, but he will be here shortly."

A simple enough statement, only that it's the voice itself that throws me off. It is the unmistakably strange and powerful voice of Donovan Rushing, Eddie Blake's partner in the restaurant and one of the most prolific chefs of the past twenty years.

Chef Rushing takes a seat beside me and I politely ask him if I may toss a few questions his way while we wait for Eddie Blake. Surprisingly, he says yes. Two birds, I suppose.

"I'm not very familiar with your magazine," he says bluntly. "But you've been publishing for a few years and to my knowledge you've never printed anything bad about me."

I thank him graciously, and jump

right in.

Coolinary Times: Hellfire Grub has become one of the premiere eateries in New York City. You are primarily known for more upscale, haute cuisine. How did you get involved in this restaurant with Eddie Blake?

Donovan Rushing: Eddie and I shared a manager, Gordon Hessler, who as you know disappeared a little over a year ago. Eddie and I sort of hit it off, which was unprecedented I assure you. We were both really tired of the whole television scene, and Eddie had this idea for a new restaurant. I was in the mood, in the state of mind, to get back into the restaurant world, and I liked his plan. So I agreed to front the money and get the ball rolling.

Coolinary Times: The restaurant was opened just a few months later. How did you two manage to get everything together so quickly?

Donovan Rushing: Well, son, when you've been around as long as I have, you make a lot of contacts in a lot of places. That helps.

Coolinary Times: Touching upon the disappearance of your manager, has any progress been made in the case?

Donovan Rushing: The last I heard, no. I personally don't believe that he will ever be found. Gordon was not the cleanest businessman. He had a number of enemies, supposedly, and I believe he owed a lot of people a lot of money. This is what I've come to learn over the last year anyway. Honestly, he could be right under your nose and you'd probably never know.

Coolinary Times: You are no stranger to unsolved mysteries.

Donovan Rushing: No. My wife's death in 1975 is still officially unsolved.

Coolinary Times: Does that still affect you?

Donovan Rushing: To an extent. But it was so long ago, you know. You sort of have to move on after a point, or it will drive you mad. I struggled with alcohol addiction for years, as a direct result. But

I'm proud to say that I have been sober for fifteen months now.

Coolinary Times: Congratulations.

Chef Rushing thanks me, and we both turn, distracted by the sound of a door opening as Eddie Blake finally walks in, apologizing for his tardiness. Chef Blake looks different since I last saw him on one of his television cooking and travel shows. His long, tangled hair is now cut shorter, his moustache and goatee are much thicker, longer. That black leather chef's coat he used to wear in promotional photographs hasn't been seen in years, but still this man is the epitome of cool. Wearing a Cramps t-shirt under a denim blazer, Chef Blake invites me into the kitchen to start the interview. Luckily, Donovan Rushing tags along.

"Brad and Angelina are coming tonight," Chef Blake says as he half-inspects the countertops in the shiny metallic Hellfire Grub kitchen. "It's their first visit, and I hope to impress."

Hellfire Grub is a virtual celebrity hang-out. Everyone from Bill Clinton to

Lou Reed to Nick Cage are regulars here. But Eddie points out that he desires to impress everyone who comes to dine here. He's made it clear since the opening that there will be no reservations. It is strictly first come, first serve. And no new patrons admitted after 11:15 PM. If you can't get in today, better luck tomorrow.

"The same will go for Brad and Angelina," he says. "If they can't get in, there's a Lobster King just up the street."

"Or Rushing's," Donovan adds, lightly chuckling to himself.

Soon after, we are seated in the dining room. The walls are dark, covered in prints of paintings by Francis Bacon and Goya. There is something ominous, sinful about the place. The seats are blood red, and the tables dark cherry wood. We are served appetizers. Cheese sticks. Simple enough, you might think. I did. Until I bit into one. Sharp cheddar sticks wrapped in Prosciutto, then dipped in batter with a parmesan crust, fried in olive oil and served with a sweet and zesty marinara sauce. I am blown away. This is delicious. Incredible. Not at all what I would expect from a place called Hellfire Grub.

While waiting for our meals, Chef Blake relaxes himself in his seat, with a glass of beer. I have a glass of white wine. Donovan Rushing is drinking a Sprite.

Coolinary Times: Just to get it out of the way, there are no illegal ingredients in any of the dishes here, right?

Eddie Blake: (laughs) No. I might have a pot brownie now and then at a friend's house, but nothing like that will be found here. We do, however, offer absinthe at the bar.

Coolinary Times: Absinthe regulations have, of course, been relaxed since 2007, so it's not outlawed in the United States any longer.

Eddie Blake: The real stuff is still illegal, but ours is the kind without the wormwood. If we could get the real thing, we'd have it, but that's as far as I would push the legal boundaries of the restaurant.

Coolinary Times: I was talking to Chef

Rushing earlier about your former manager, Gordon Hessler, whose disappearance more than a year ago is still unsolved.

Eddie Blake: That was a very strange time in my life. A twisted sort of transition period. I was, I don't know, going in a few different directions at once. The thing with Gordon certainly made things a little more weird.

Coolinary Times: You had signed on to co-host Chef Rushing's show (*The Main Course with Donovan Rushing*).

Eddie Blake: Yes. But it was doomed from the start. Neither Donovan and I were interested in doing television anymore. He had been doing the same show for twenty years. More than that really. I had been jumping around, from dumb show to stupid show. I wasn't really cut out for television. I couldn't do the same things for too long. Sooner or later I would have ended up destroying Donovan's show.

Donovan Rushing: So I decided to destroy it myself, before he got the chance. (laughs)

Coolinary Times: The disappearance of your manager played a part in your decision to end the show?

Donovan Rushing: When Gordon vanished, there was a week or so of absolute chaos. Gordon controlled so much behind the scenes, I really never had any idea, call me naïve. And now, every producer and his brother were trying to fill his space. Trying to grab the wheel and steer the ship. But the ship wasn't going anywhere anymore. It was on dry land. So I just left the ship and found a new place to waste my precious time.

Eddie Blake: I was very fortunate in that Donovan did not leave me out in the rain. Truth be told, we did not hit if off at the beginning.

Coolinary Times: Is that so?

Eddie Blake: Sure. Donovan had been a solo act for his whole life. And here I was, this captain weirdo cook just strutting into his world.

Donovan Rushing: I really thought about

killing you a few times. (both laugh) I really hated you.

Eddie Blake: It's a good thing you are all bark.

Donovan Rushing: I really couldn't harm a fly. (Both laugh, even louder)

Eddie then starts on how the restaurant came together. The opening night jitters. The usual filler you get during these interviews. But I am just waiting for something more. Something interesting. This is Eddie Blake we're talking about here. And Donovan Rushing. There has to be something amazing to learn from these two. And then, the food arrives.

I have a plate of barbeque pork ribs, with a side of roasted garlic mashed potatoes and Texas toast. Dear god. I have tasted the forbidden fruit. And it is good. And perhaps this is the point. Eddie Blake, the great American rebel chef has grown up and created what may just be the best restaurant in New York City. He has found his place, and it works.

Coolinary Times: What's the flavor in this barbeque sauce? Is that apple?

Chef Blake just smiles. And then another round of food. This time, it's the famous Mystery Meat Stew that they serve on rare occasions. I am astonished. It's so hot. More like a chili, but with fresh vegetables. No one knows what the meat is, and no one cares. My guess is pork. Something imported.

It is the most delicious thing I have ever had in my mouth.

"You are one of the last few people who will ever eat that stew," Chef Blake says.

I am honored, I tell him. And I really am. I had no idea, when accepting this assignment that I would have this incredible experience. This nearly life changing meal. It's like meeting Hitler. Or sleeping with the quarterback's girlfriend. Exciting. Scary. Borderline crazy. Personally historic.

As the dessert arrives, shiny little fresh baked lemon squares, Donovan

Rushing excuses himself from the table to make a phone call. I take this opportunity to ask a few personal questions of Eddie Blake.

Coolinary Times: So, is it true that you had an affair with Giada De Laurentiis?

Eddie Blake: (laughs) The tabloids love that kind of stuff. I thought you guys were above that.

Coolinary Times: Okay, here's a better one. Is Donovan Rushing really as crazy as everyone thinks?

Eddie Blake leans in close to whisper. "Honestly.. He is the craziest person I have ever met in my life. But you know what? I wouldn't have him any other way."

A shot glass of ice cold milk and vodka caps off the desert, and the meal is over. I thank Eddie Blake for his time and hospitality. I leave a generous tip, and I make my way towards the door. On my way out, I see Chefs Rushing and Blake, huddling up in the kitchen doorway.

They look towards me, and begin to laugh. I check my shirt. Did I spill barbeque sauce? No. Is there lemon on my chin? No. Just an insignificant inside joke, I guess.

Then again, everything in this world is just part of one massive insignificant inside joke. You just have to be cool enough to know the punch line. Chefs Blake and Rushing obviously know the punch line. So I say, let them have their laughs.

I'll just have their food.

Conrad Mizelli is a Coolinary Times *special correspondent.*

THE MAIN COURSE COOKBOOK

So you wanna cook like Donovan Rushing and Eddie Blake, eh? Too bad. Those guys are about as good as you can get. But perhaps you can cook like me, Chuck Morgue. I'm not great. But I don't suck either. And that should be just fine.

I am going to offer a few recipes that I like. A few are basics, a few are pretty intricate. But if you're patient, nothing is too hard to prepare.

I have a few rules to go over before we begin.

First, you need to make sure your kitchen is clean. So clean it up. Wash your pans and forks. Make that shit shine. You have to eat off that stuff.

Second, go buy some extra virgin olive oil. I don't want to sound like Rachel Ray, but really, it is the nectar of the gods as far as cooking is concerned.

Third, only cook what you are going to eat. If the idea of a spinach and liver quiche sounds disgusting to you (it does to me) then don't bother. Stick to pork chops.

Or grilled cheese sandwiches.

And fourth, get a fucking radio. Music makes this shit go by much quicker, and adds to the enjoyment. I prefer to cook to The Ramones, or Queen. Maybe a little Johnny Cash. Forget about Slayer, you'll get your ingredients all over the goddamn place.

I really would love to see more people getting into the kitchen to cook. Fewer and fewer younger people are getting involved in cooking for themselves, relying on McDonalds and KFC for their "nutrition."

That's a real fucking shame, kids. Put down that Whopper. Grab a grill and make your own.

Anyway, I hope you'll try some of these. I'm sure you'll have fun.

~~Chuck Morgue

PASTA DOUGH

Ingredients:
3 ½ cups all-purpose flour, plus extra for kneading
5 large eggs

Instructions:
Mound the flour in the center of a large wooden board. Make a well in the center of the flour with your finger and add the eggs. Using a fork, beat the eggs together and then begin to incorporate the flour, starting with the inner rim of the well. As you expand the well, keep pushing the flour up to retain the well shape (do not worry if it looks messy). When half of the flour is incorporated, the dough will begin to come together. Start kneading the dough, using primarily the palms of your hands. Once the dough is a cohesive mess, set the dough aside and scrape up and discard any dried bits of dough.

Lightly flour the board and continue kneading for 10 minutes, dusting the board with additional flour as necessary. The dough should be elastic and a little sticky. Wrap the dough in plastic wrap and allow to rest for 30 minutes at room temperature before using. You'll end up with about 1 ¼ pound of dough. You can divide it up, roll it flat (very flat) and cut with a knife. Or buy a pasta maker to feed the dough into and you can make any pasta. Angel hair. Fettuccini. Lasagna. Ravioli. You can even use the dough for pizza crust.

You are almost certain to make a mess with this shit, at least the first few times. We can't all be Mario Batali. Especially me, my hair is not red. And I'm not nearly as cool. Even though I try to fake it.

ALFREDO SAUCE

Ingredients:
¼ cup butter
1 cup heavy cream
1 clove garlic, crushed
1 ½ cups freshly grated Parmesan cheese
¼ cup chopped fresh parsley

Instructions:
Melt butter in medium saucepan over medium heat. Add cream and simmer for 5 minutes. Add garlic and cheese and whisk quickly, heating through. Stir in parsley and serve.

Adding chicken, shrimp or pork to the sauce, and serving with fettuccini is highly recommended. Especially the pork. Yes.

ROASTED GARLIC

Ingredients:
4 cloves of garlic.
½ cup of chicken broth.
2 tablespoons of butter.
½ teaspoon of dried leaf thyme.
¼ teaspoon of ground black pepper.
¼ teaspoon of salt.

Instructions:
Remove the outer peel from the garlic. Place the garlic cloves in a baking dish. Dab each clove with butter. Sprinkle the garlic cloves with thyme, pepper and salt. Pour the chicken broth into the dish.
Cover the dish with foil and bake at 350°F (175°C) for one hour, basting frequently. Uncover the dish and bake at the same temperature for another 15 minutes.

You can pretty much put this shit in anything, and it will improve the meal. I believe it was Anthony Bourdain who once said, and I'm paraphrasing here, "There is not a dish in the world that you can add bacon to and not make the dish better." Well for me, there's no dish that garlic will not make better.

PORK ROAST WITH HERBED PEPPER RUB

Ingredients:
1 3-pound boneless pork loin roast
3 tablespoons freshly cracked black pepper
2 tablespoons grated Parmesan cheese
2 teaspoons dried basil
2 teaspoons dried rosemary
2 teaspoons dried thyme
1/4 teaspoon garlic powder
1/4 teaspoon salt

Instructions:
Pat pork dry with paper towel. In small bowl, combine all rub ingredients well and apply to all surfaces of the pork roast. Place roast in a shallow pan and roast in a 350 degrees F. oven for 1-1 1/4 hours (18-20 minutes per pound), until internal temperature, measured with a meat thermometer, registers 155 degrees F. Remove roast from oven and let rest for 5-10 minutes before slicing to serve. Serves 6-8, with leftovers. Absolutely one of my favorite fucking things to make (and eat). I LOVE pork. And this oh so tender loin is my personal comfort food. I usually add more black pepper, my favorite seasoning.

GARLIC CHEESE CHICKEN ROLLUPS

Ingredients:
4 skinless, boneless chicken breasts
1 cup dried bread crumbs, seasoned
1/2 cup grated Parmesan cheese
1/4 cup butter, melted
1 (7 ounce) package garlic cheese spread

Instructions:
Preheat oven to 350 degrees F (175 degrees C).

Pound chicken breasts until thinned out. In a shallow dish or bowl mix together bread crumbs and cheese. Dip one side of each breast into melted butter or margarine, then into crumb/cheese mixture. Place a dollop of cheese spread at one end of each chicken breast, on the side of the breast not dipped in the mixture. Roll up each breast and secure with toothpicks.

Place rollups in a lightly greased 9x13 inch baking dish and drizzle any remaining butter or margarine over all. Bake in the preheated oven for 35 to 40 minutes, or until cooked through and juices run clear.

The only thing more awesome than garlic is cheese. So putting them together along with some tasty ass chicken.. Come on, you know you want this shit.

CHILI

Ingredients:
1 lb lean ground meat (I prefer ground pork)
1 Large can of stewed tomatoes
1 small can of tomato paste
1 large onion
5 cloves garlic
2 Tablespoons freshly ground black pepper
1 Tablespoon ground cumin
1 Tablespoon onion powder
1 Tablespoon Paprika
1 Tablespoon Oregano
1 Tablespoon salt
3 Tablespoons chili powder
Red Pepper (Cayenne)

Instructions:
Brown meat in large pan. When the meat is nearly done, stir in the onion and garlic and continue stirring until the meat is done and the onions/garlic are becoming transparent.

Gently stir in tomato paste, stewed tomatoes, undrained beans, and the other dry ingredients. Chop the stewed tomatoes with your spoon (they're really soft) as you continue to stir in the ingredients.

Add Red pepper (Cayenne) to taste--as much as you think you can handle (see heat scale). Simmer at least 30 minutes. Chili will thicken as it simmers. To increase evaporation, heat without a lid. Simmer at least 15 minutes on LOW heat. Makes about a gallon of Chili! Some people like to add beans to their chili, I don't. You can do whatever the fuck you want. Chili is practically foolproof. If you can't make chili, you should stick to bologna sandwiches.

DINNER ROLLS

Ingredients:
1 cup warm water
2 packages active dry yeast
½ cup or 1 stick butter, melted
½ cup sugar
3 eggs
1 teaspoon salt
4 ½ cups all-purpose flour

Instructions:
Combine warm water and yeast in a large mixing bowl. Let stand for about 5 minutes, until yeast is foamy. Stir in butter, eggs, sugar and salt. Beat in flour, 1 cup at a time, until dough is too tough to mix (some of the flour may not be needed). Cover with plastic wrap and refrigerate for at least 2 hours.

Grease a 13x9-inch baking pan. Put the chilled dough out on a lightly floured board. Divide the dough into 24 equal-size pieces. Roll each piece into a smooth round ball, and place them in even rows in the baking pan. Cover and let dough balls rise until doubled in volume, approximately 1 hour.

Preheat oven to 375° F. Bake 15-20

minutes, or until rolls are golden brown. You can smear butter all over the rolls if you like (I prefer a honey butter spread). Then tear these babies apart and pass them around. You just made some new friends.

GARLIC POTATO PIE

Ingredients:
1 lb of scrubbed boiling potatoes.
6 cloves fresh garlic, sliced finely.
1 cup of milk.
¼ cup of breadcrumbs.
3 tablespoons of grated parmesan cheese.
3 tablespoons of butter.

Instructions:
Preheat your oven to 380° F.

Slice potatoes thinly. Butter a 9-inch pie plate. Arrange a layer of potatoes, garlic slices, parmesan and slices of butter.

Repeat using the rest of the ingredients (other than the milk), saving some of the cheese and the butter. Heat the milk and pour over top of the potatoes. Top with bread crumbs and remaining cheese and butter.

Bake for 1 hour, until the potatoes are tender and top has turned golden brown. A simple dish that goes with almost anything. Serve it with that pork loin roast.

PORK CHOPS WRAPPED IN PROSCIUTTO

Ingredients:
6 bone in, center cut pork chops
1/4 pound of thinly sliced Parma Prosciutto
1 tablespoon fresh rosemary leaves, rough chop
1 tablespoon fresh sage leaves, rough chop
1/4 tablespoon freshly crushed black pepper
1/4 cup extra virgin olive oil

Instructions:
Preheat oven to 375 to 400° F. Center cut pork chops should be at least 1½-inches thick and fat trimmed away from bone. Season each side of pork chop evenly with rosemary, sage and cracked black pepper. (Note: Do not season with salt due to Prosciutto's salty nature).

Take 2 pieces of thinly sliced Prosciutto and wrap one continuous band around each pork chop until Prosciutto meets. After all pork chops have been wrapped, heat 10-inch, preferably non-stick sauté pan, to medium-high heat and brown pork chops evenly on both sides (approximately 2 minutes).

Place all pork chops on sheet pan and cook in preheated oven for approximately 15 to 20 minutes for medium; 30 minutes for well down.

Mmm.. Pork wrapped in more pork. I should have worked in some garlic into this recipe, but that might be overkill with the garlic. Now, how about something for the sweet side of the table.

MOLTEN CHOCOLATE CAKE

Ingredients:
2 Tablespoons plus ¾ cup of butter (or, 1 ½ sticks)
8 oz. 62% bittersweet baking chocolate, broken into pieces
3 large eggs
3 large egg yolks
¼ cup plus 1 Tablespoon granulated sugar
1 teaspoon vanilla extract
1 Tablespoon all-purpose flour

Instructions:
Preheat oven to 425° F. Butter six 6-ounce ramekins with two tablespoons of butter.

Stir ¾ cup butter and chocolate in medium saucepan over low heat until chocolate is melted. Remove from heat. Beat eggs, egg yolks, sugar and vanilla extract in large bowl until thick. Let sit for 8 minutes. Gently fold 1/3 of the melted chocolate into the egg mix, until well blended. Fold in remaining chocolate and flour until well blended. Divide batter among the prepared ramekins and place on baking sheet.

Bake for 12 to 13 minutes or until side are

set and 1-inch centers move slightly when shaken. Remove from oven and place on rack.

When ready to serve, use a thin knife around the top edge of the cakes to loosen them up. Gently, VERY FUCKING GENTLY, set the cakes upside down onto serving plates,and lift off the ramekins.

And now dig in with a fork. Watch that gooey chocolate spill from the center. I dare you not to get turned on.

THE MAIN COURSE TRAILER

Pardon me. Hello. I'm sorry, but I noticed you sitting here and I thought I should introduce myself.

My name is Donovan Rushing. Perhaps you have heard of me. I'm one of those celebrity chefs you always see on television showing you how to make exquisitely delicious meals in under an hour.

Step One: Rinse off the meat and remove the skin.

Well, I have a problem. You see, ever since my cooking show moved from New York to Los Angeles, I have had the undeniable feeling that I am losing control over my life. Everyone, it would seem, is out to get me. From the producers to the assistants, to the autograph hounds to the haute cuisine food addicts.

I can see it in their eyes. They want me. They want what I have. And they are all scheming to take it from me.

*Step Two: Fillet the meat. Season with extra
virgin olive oil and red pepper flakes.*

My manager Gordon Hessler says that I have been working too hard. And drinking too much. Although I can hardly believe that a few glasses (bottles?) of wine a day could be considered excessive. And besides, I'm starting to think that maybe he is in on it too.

Gordon recently signed a new client, this crazy hippie MTV chef named Eddie Blake. And the network is trying to add him to my TV program. Against my wishes. They say that they are interested in attracting a younger, more in touch, audience. Bullshit if you ask me. The hippie is probably behind the whole thing. Trying to take over my show, and commandeer my cooking empire.

*Step Three: Place fillets in pan over medium
heat. Approximately 4 minutes per side.*

Everyone says I should slow down. Take a break.

They all think that I am crazy, you know. And maybe I am. But that wouldn't make me wrong in my assumptions. Maybe they are all making me crazy. Then they can just toss me aside.

Well fuck them. Fuck them all.

Step Four: Place meat on plate with garnish. Slice meat down center.

Donovan Rushing makes the rules, god dammit. Donovan Rushing calls the shots.

Anyway. I'm sorry about that. Would you like to get a drink. I know a guy downtown who'll let me drink for free all night.

Step Five: Don't be afraid of the blood. It's perfectly natural.

Just look me in the eyes and tell me that I'm not fucking crazy.

Step Six: Bon Appétit.

****

From the author of the chilling 2007 horror novella *The Horns Of Evangelina* comes a bloody tale of murder, conspiracy, and gourmet excellence that reaches from Los Angeles to New York to Paris and beyond.

Delve into the madness and mystery of **CHUCK MORGUE**'s new novel

THE MAIN COURSE

A seven-course meal of sociopathic extremity

Coming soon from HOUSE OF MORGUE

www.houseofmorgue.com
www.myspace.com/houseofmorgue

AFTERWORD: THE LIST

So I wanted to end this book in the proper way. The respectful way. And I thought to myself, so many great authors and books were raped by me just to write *The Main Course*, the least I could do is give some props. So I decided to do this recommended reading list to share with you these books, all of which were influential and helpful to me in writing *The Main Course*. It is a collection of fiction and nonfiction, most having to do with food, chefs, travel, and mystery.

My intention is to turn you on to the books that gave me so much enjoyment. So much inspiration during the year I spent working on *The Main Course*. All of these books are currently in print, and you should read them all.

The first two books I must recommend are *Liquor* (2004, fiction) by Poppy Z. Brite and **Kitchen Confidential** (2000, nonfiction) by Anthony Bourdain. These two books were the most influential to me. If it weren't for Poppy Z. Brite's *Liquor* series of books I may have never found myself interested in culinary fiction.

And I am hopelessly addicted to anything bearing Anthony Bourdain's name, not just for his memoirs about his cooking career, but because he is simply one of the absolute coolest people on Earth. His Travel Channel series *Anthony Bourdain: No Reservations* is one of my can't-miss shows.

Michael Ruhlman's **The Reach Of A Chef** (2006, nonfiction) was indispensable to me during the writing of this book. Not being familiar with the restaurant world myself, his outsider approach to his book was extremely helpful.

Joseph Suglia's raunchy and twisted novel **Watch Out** (2006, fiction) was influential in my decision to write a more realistic, first-person narrative that dealt with peculiar psychological issues. Joseph's friendship and supportive criticism during the last year have been greatly appreciated. Go buy his book now.

Heat (2006, nonfiction) by Bill Buford was also a useful guide to the culinary world which I was just beginning to familiarize myself with. And it showed to me that Chef Mario Batali is also in that Bourdain league of really fucking cool people.

If *The Reach Of A Chef* and *Heat* were my unofficial encyclopedias during my writing of *The Main Course*, then **The Food Snob's Dictionary** (2007, nonfiction) by David Kamp and Marion Rosenfeld was certainly my dictionary. With humor and sharp wit, Kamp and Rosenfeld's little book served as my beginners guide to the lexicon and vernacular of the foodie world. I even took advantage of **The Complete Idiot's Guide To Cooking Basics** (1995, nonfiction) by Ronnie Fein. Hey, I grabbed everything within reach.

You should keep an eye out for **Stanley Park** (2001, fiction) by Timothy Taylor. It was one of those few culinary novels I found that successfully crossed genre lines to tell an amazing and mysterious story.

I recommend the other books in Poppy Z. Brite's *Liquor* series: ***The Value Of X*** (2003, fiction), ***Prime*** (2005, fiction) and ***Soul Kitchen*** (2006, fiction) and I pray to every god imaginable that she'll start feeling better soon and put out new books in this, my absolute favorite literary series.

After this, all that is left is countless books by countless authors. David Sedaris. Bret Easton Ellis. Gordon Ramsay. Charles Bukowski. Oscar Wilde. Really, everything I have ever read, whether I enjoyed it or not, will find it's way into my writing.

In a way, *The Main Course* is sort of my real literary debut, since it was directly inspired by other literature. My 2007 horror novella *The Horns Of Evangelina* was inspired by thirty years of exploitation horror cinema. The closest I had to a literary influence for that book was some of Clive Barker's early writing. Maybe some H.P. Lovecraft. Certainly nothing I could definitely put my finger on (okay, Mary Shelley's *Frankenstein*, but that's it).

I am proud of the fact that I took advantage of so many specific literary influences in crafting *The Main Course*. And so is my muse. She ate very well over the last year.

I offer my sincerest gratitude to these authors not only for their inspiration, but for their entertainment. Even if I had never written *The Main Course*, their books would still have enlightened me, would still resonate within my mind on a daily basis.

And I can't forget about all those Christopher Walken and Johnny Depp movies I watched. I don't know how much of the personalities of these two extraordinary men made it into my characters Donovan Rushing and Eddie Blake, but I had a lot of fun watching those films over and over again.

Let's just hope that I have not offended them. I would hate to get sued by the two actors I admire most (even though, it would actually be kind of cool).

When you get right down to it, this book is essentially a love letter to Anthony Bourdain, Poppy Z. Brite, Christopher

Walken and Johnny Depp. The coolest mother fuckers in the world.

Thank you, dear reader for picking up my book *The Main Course*. Do yourself a favor, and pick up a few of these other books I have recommended. I loved them, and I'm sure you will too.

~ Chuck Morgue
December 2008
Somewhere in southwest Louisiana

CHUCK MORGUE is a writer and artist living with his wife and children in a secret bunker in southern Louisiana. His first book, *THE HORNS OF EVANGELINA*, was an underground horror hit. He also enjoys macramé, yacht-detailing, plagiarism and long walks through dark and dangerous neighborhoods.

www.ingramcontent.com/pod-product-compliance
Lightning Source LLC
Chambersburg PA
CBHW031200020726
47499CB00002B/434